THE UNSEEN

Scary Stories

Selected by

J A N E T   L U N N

Stoddart

*Stoddart Publishing gratefully acknowledges the support
of the Canada Council and the Ontario Arts Council in the
development of writing and publishing in Canada.*

First published in 1994 by Lester Publishing Limited.

Published in 1996 by
Stoddart Publishing Co. Limited
34 Lesmill Road
Toronto, Canada M3B 2T6
Tel. (416) 445-3333
Fax (416) 445-5967
e-mail Customer.Service@ccmailgw.genpub.com

Canadian Cataloguing in Publication Data

Main entry under title:
The unseen: scary stories

ISBN 0-7737-5845-3

I. Ghost stories, Canadian (English).
I. Lunn, Janet, 1928–

PS8323.G5U5 1996   C813'.0873308   C96-990025-2
PR9197.35.G45U5 1996

Printed and bound in Canada

To the kind lady who haunts my house,
whoever she is

– J. L.

CONTENTS

Janet Lunn

FOREWORD

Ghosts. Unseen presences. Shapes lingering in the shadows. No matter how many people tell us there are no such things, we know that the lingering shapes, the unseen presences, have a reality we cannot dismiss. When I was three or four years old, my older sister recited this poem to me:

> As I was going up the stair,
> I met a man who wasn't there.
> He wasn't there again today.
> Oh, how I wish he'd go away.

My sister meant to frighten me, but in a way, she comforted me. I knew that man. He — or someone very like him — lurked in the dark just behind my closet door. Hearing that verse confirmed my sense of what was true. I never saw the man, but I knew he was there. I have never seen a ghost either, but now I live in a house with one.

My house is old for Ontario. The oldest part of it was built around 1820, the newest around 1900. A lot of people have lived here in all those years. They have left behind their memories, their feelings, maybe even their shadows. One of them appeared to my husband the year we moved in — a friendly old lady, we think.

No one knows for sure just what ghosts are. Some may be memories, some time crossings, some hallucinations, some odd creatures we only ever catch a glimpse of from the corner of an eye.

This book is full of stories and poems about ghosts in Canada. Some are the ghosts we expect to find, all misty and spooky, while others are more unusual. One we would not think of as a ghost at all if we were to look at the story backward.

I hope you will enjoy reading these stories as much as I enjoyed collecting them.

Archibald Lampman

MIDNIGHT

From where I sit, I see the stars,
  And down the chilly floor
The moon between the frozen bars
  Is glimmering dim and hoar.

Without in many a peakèd mound
  The glinting snowdrifts lie;
There is no voice or living sound;
  The embers slowly die.

Yet some wild thing is in mine ear;
  I hold my breath and hark;
Out of the depth I seem to hear
  A crying in the dark:

No sound of man or wife or child,
  No sound of beast that groans,
Or of the wind that whistles wild,
  Or of the tree that moans:

I know not what it is I hear;
  I bend my head and hark:
I cannot drive it from mine ear,
  That crying in the dark.

Joyce Barkhouse

HAUNTED ISLAND

Far off the shores of Nova Scotia lies Sable Island, the graveyard of the Atlantic. On this treacherous desert in the sea no trees grow. Wild horses shelter behind towering dunes, feed on the rich marram grass, and find fresh water in a small inland lake. Herds of seals bask on the beaches all summer. The animals share the island peacefully but humans have chilling tales to tell; tales not only of the violence of the sea but also of human violence and of the lost souls who haunt these desolate shores.

Sable Island is not a quiet place. Even on calm days there is the constant sound of breakers, and when the sky turns black and a sudden storm springs up, the noise is terrifying. Sometimes, above the tumult, voices can be heard.

There is one, they say, who moans and complains in French about the king who banished his wife to Sable. In life the stricken husband followed her, meaning to share her exile, but when he reached the island, she was dead. He died of grief soon after, but his ghost unceasingly, neverendingly, curses the king who caused his torment. There is, too, the murderer of a Portuguese king. He escaped punishment only to live out his days in misery on Sable Island. His ghost wears a broad-brimmed hat and sings psalms in Portuguese in an unearthly nasal voice. But the most famous and maybe the saddest of all the ghosts on Sable Island is Annie Copeland, who died almost two hundred years ago.

The year was 1800 and she was first seen by a friend, a man named Torrens, a captain in the British Army who was stationed in Halifax. He had been ordered by the duke of Kent, also stationed in Halifax, to sail to Sable Island to investigate the circumstances of the wreck of *The Francis*.

In December of the previous year *The Francis*, on its way from London, England, to Halifax with the valuable equipage of the duke, had been driven ashore in a hurricane. Every soul on board had perished. Lately, however, jewels and other precious articles had been seen in the cottages of Nova Scotia fishermen. There were people who said these things had come from Sable Island. They whispered tales of vicious pirates and of murder, and claimed that not all aboard *The Francis* had drowned. Some had reached shore safely, they said, only to be killed mercilessly for the sake of their possessions.

Taking with him his dog, Whiskey, Captain Torrens set sail for Sable Island on the brig *Hariot*, determined to find any pirates who might be lurking there, any evidence of foul play. He had had friends on *The Francis*, a Dr. and Mrs. Copeland, and he wanted to make sure, personally, that they had not met the fate so many feared.

Then the *Hariot*, too, was wrecked on Sable Island and many of its crew were drowned. Torrens himself nearly lost his life trying to save others. Those left alive managed to salvage enough food to survive for a few weeks. Then they set about the melancholy duty of burying their dead comrades. Deeply depressed, Torrens left them to their grisly task and set off with his dog to explore the east end of the island.

He ventured too far and twilight came sooner than he expected. Luckily he discovered a rough hut near the island's lake. Inside he found a fireplace and a pile of driftwood for fuel. There were no signs of recent occupation, so he built a fire, ate the cheese he had in his pocket, and curled up in a corner on a bed of grass. In spite of the booming of the breakers on the beaches and the moaning of the wind, he fell asleep at once.

He was awakened suddenly by a deep growl from the dog. He sat up. There, seated before the embers of his fire, was a young woman. Her long hair hung heavy and wet over her shoulders and all but covered her face. She wore only a soiled white dress, which was as wet as her hair.

"Good heavens, Madam! Where did you come from?" Torrens exclaimed.

She did not answer. She only held up her left hand. The captain saw that one of her fingers had been cut off. It was dripping blood.

He jumped up. Frantically he looked around him to find something to use as a bandage. In that moment the air about him turned cold as ice, and in a single movement, the woman rose and slipped past him through the door.

For a moment the captain just stared, then he ran after her. But she was as swift as the wind. It was a clear, moonlit night, and to his horror, he saw her dive, head first, into the lake. The dog raced after her, whining and barking, but a moment later, when the captain reached the water's edge, there wasn't even a ripple to show where the woman had disappeared.

"I must be insane. The sight of all those dead bodies this morning has unbalanced my mind," he thought.

He slowly returned to the hut with Whiskey trotting by his side. When they came to the door, the dog stopped. He began to growl and refused to go inside. Torrens saw the hackles rise along the dog's back. He looked inside and felt his own hair prickle on the nape of his neck.

There was the young woman sitting by the fireplace. Fearfully the captain entered. He approached her cautiously, and as he drew near, she turned and held up her mutilated hand. This time he saw her face. It was as white as the moon, but he knew her.

"Why, Annie Copeland, it's you!" he cried.

She bowed her head, still holding up the stump of her bleeding finger. Suddenly Torrens understood. He remembered the beautiful ring Annie Copeland had always worn, had always treasured so greatly. It had an unusual design set with rubies and diamonds. It had been much admired by her friends in Halifax.

"I know what you are trying to tell me. You were murdered for your ring," he whispered.

She stood and, once more, slipped past him through the door. This time he knew it was useless to follow. He lay down on his bed of grass, but he could not sleep. He vowed that, when he returned to the mainland, he would bring Annie Copeland's murderer to justice.

No pirates were found on the island. In fact, nothing was found to show there had ever been any pirates there. But when the survivors from the wrecked *Hariot* were rescued, Torrens was given a leave of absence to learn what he could about Annie Copeland's ring.

What he learned was that a man in Barrington on the South Shore had been selling rich and unlikely goods in his village. Men in the area were wearing soldiers' caps and red coats, women were cutting up finery to make quilts.

These poor, isolated fisherfolk were glad to get anything to help eke out a living. They asked few questions.

Captain Torrens went to Barrington with the pretense of being on a hunting and fishing holiday. He found a place to board, and as soon as he'd become friendly with the family, he began to ask questions. And yes, they had heard about a fisherman in Salmon River who had come into possession of a gorgeous jeweled ring.

Torrens rode at once to Salmon River, only to discover that the man he wanted was away at sea. However, his wife was friendly. She showed Torrens where to tether his horse and invited him into her house for a cup of tea.

Three of the woman's daughters were sitting by the fire with their sewing. A baby was playing on the floor. The girls glanced at Torrens shyly, but the baby came to him at once and put a hand on his knee. He pulled his signet ring from his finger as if to entertain the baby and then held it up for the others to see.

"I greatly value this ring," he told them. "It's very useful. When I write a letter, I press my ring into the soft sealing wax. The wax then bears the imprint of my family's coat of arms."

As he had hoped, one of the girls held out her hand for the ring. She examined it critically. "It's nice," she agreed, "but it ain't nearly so pretty as the one Pa brought home from Sable Island. It sparkled with diamonds and . . ."

"Nonsense!" Her mother interrupted angrily. "It wan't but a cheap bit of a thing. Somethin' he picked up from a beach around here."

"Oh ... oh ... yes ... I ..." the girl stammered.

The captain put his ring back on his finger. "I'd like to see your ring. If it is as beautiful as the girl says, I might like to buy the bauble as a gift for my wife."

"Oh, we don't got it no more," said one of the younger girls. "Pa took it to a watchmaker up in Halifax to sell it."

Torrens drank his tea, thanked them for their hospitality, and returned to Halifax at once.

There weren't many watchmakers in Halifax in 1800 and he had no trouble finding the ring from Salmon River. He had no trouble recognizing it, either. It was, indeed, Annie Copeland's ring. When the watchmaker heard the story, he was glad to be rid of the stolen property. He was anxious not to get into trouble with the law.

Captain Torrens sent the ring to Annie Copeland's family in England. However, for reasons known only to himself, he did not pursue the fisherman from Salmon River. Perhaps he felt sorry for the family, who were working so hard to make their small living. In any case, the criminal was never brought to justice.

But the tale of Annie Copeland's ghost was told all over Nova Scotia and people in Salmon River began to avoid the pirate. He lived in fear the rest of his life, afraid even to step outside his door after dark.

Eventually the tale came to the ears of Sir John Wentworth, governor of the colony. He had heard other shocking stories about the pirates of Sable Island. He wrote to the authorities in England and told them of "the unfeeling persons who have chosen to winter there" and of those who "had been deprived of their lives by beings more merciless than the waves."

In 1801 an act was passed by the British government to ensure the removal of pirates from Sable Island. Life-saving stations were built there and men on horseback patrolled the shores regularly. In modern times radar has made them unnecessary.

It is said that, through those long, lonely years, more than one patrolman heard ghostly voices and saw the pale lady with the missing finger pass swiftly before him through the mist and swirling sands, only to disappear without a ripple into the waters of the lake.

• • •

Kit Pearson

MISS KIRKPATRICK'S SECRET

Abbie stood in front of the shabby old house with her two older brothers. In spite of the sunny morning, all the windows had dark curtains pulled across them. They stared back at her blindly. Rustling sounds came from under the unraked leaves behind the picket fence.

"O-o-o-o. . . ." Michael moaned in her ear.

"Isn't it *spooky*?" whispered Kyle. "I think it's haunted — don't you, Abbie?"

"Stop it!" Abbie shivered. They were always trying to scare her and she was always mad at herself for giving in. She took a deep breath. "Those are just birds in the grass. And there's no such thing as ghosts," she added loudly, to convince herself.

As long as Abbie could remember there had only been one person living in the house: old Miss Kirkpatrick. She rarely came out and she never asked anyone in.

"I bet she's a witch!" said Kyle.

"Yeah, a witch who *eats* nine-year-old girls."
Michael grinned. He lurched after Abbie. "Come here,
my luscious morsel. . . ."

Abbie screamed and ran home. Her brothers got told
off for teasing her, but as usual that didn't stop them.

"I wish you could learn to be braver, Abbie," sighed
Mum as she hugged her. "Why does everything scare you
so much?"

"I don't know," whispered Abbie. "I can't help it."
She had to be taken out of movies while younger kids sat
calmly, and every night she leapt into bed to avoid the
awful things she was sure lived underneath it.

That March, Miss Kirkpatrick died. When the next-
door neighbors had not seen her for days, they broke in
and found the old woman's body in her bed. The Edmonton newspaper said she was ninety-three, and had lived
in the house all her life. Now it stood empty, huddled at
the back of its long front yard.

On the first day of the Easter holidays Abbie took the
family dog, Bacon, for a walk. Spring had arrived. Muddy
water rushed alongside the curb, swirling with twigs and
leaves and a lost mitten. Abbie's feet felt light without
boots and her hair was hot when she touched it. Michael
and Kyle had gone skiing with their friends, so Abbie had
a whole week to choose her own TV programs and prac-
tice her ballet steps without anyone teasing her.

She walked for three blocks, passing neat bungalows

on one side and the river valley on the other. Then she paused at Miss Kirkpatrick's house. Two signs in the yard said Sold and No Trespassing. The windows, now free of curtains, had become wide-open eyes that glowered at her.

Someone died in there. . . . Abbie shuddered and started to walk on, but Bacon refused to leave. He stood at the gate, cocked his head, and whined. Then he nosed the gate open and trotted into the yard.

"Bacon!" Abbie called, but he had disappeared around the back of the house. She looked up and down the street, chewing the end of her braid. No one was around to see her trespass.

Her heart thudding, she made herself open the gate and shuffle through a carpet of rotting leaves to the backyard. It was a jungle of lilac bushes, pines, and mountain ash trees. Bacon was nowhere in sight.

Abbie called down the back lane, then returned to the yard. Beside the back door of the house, she saw another tiny door. It stood wide open. She knew what this was: a milk box. Their own house had one that was sealed up. They were used a long time ago when milk had been delivered door-to-door in Edmonton.

The little door creaked in the breeze. Abbie desperately wanted to run away, but she had to find Bacon. Her heart pounding, she forced herself to walk over to the milk box and peer in. Another little door opened into the house, and Abbie could see the linoleum floor of a kitchen. Bacon's toenails clicked at the far end of it.

"Bacon! Come back!" she entreated, but the dog ignored her. She swallowed a sob. What was the matter with him? He was usually so obedient. What would entice him to jump up and crawl through the milk box?

Abbie struggled with her terror. She was going to have to go after Bacon, but how could she enter this house that had always scared her so much? And what if somebody caught her?

Don't be such a coward, she told herself. Just do it! She clenched her fists and tried to stop shaking. Quickly, before she had time to think further, she hoisted herself up and slithered through the box with room to spare. She was not much bigger than Bacon, and a lot skinnier.

She stood up in a shadowy kitchen. At the back of it was a huge, black iron stove. A tiny refrigerator, its door open, stood in a corner. On the wall was a calendar from forty years earlier.

To her astonishment, Abbie was no longer quite as frightened. Her heart still thudded, but she felt welcome, as if the house were glad to have a visitor.

Bacon was sniffing the floor. When he saw her, he gave a worried bark and started to lead her to the milk box. But Abbie shut the little door. "Quiet, Bacon!" she whispered. She wiped her sweaty palms on her jeans and peeked through the kitchen door into the rest of the house. No one knew she was here; if she were careful, she could look around.

She crept around the empty rooms on her hands and knees, so she wouldn't be spotted from the street. The sun coming in through the dirty windows lit up dust balls and spider webs on the grimy floor. If only Michael and Kyle could see me now, thought Abbie. I bet *they'd* be scared! She was surprised that she wasn't. She felt as if someone were giving her a tour, leading her on from room to room.

Bacon came with her as she crawled up the stairs. He licked her face and pawed her shoulder anxiously. Abbie pushed him off. "Leave me alone!" she scolded. Bacon gave her a hurt look and slinked away.

Growing more excited, Abbie explored the second floor. She found three large bedrooms and a spacious bathroom with a tub big enough to float in. Part of her wanted to stop there and try lying in it, but she felt drawn as if by a magnet to the last bedroom, which was at the front of the house. It had a view overlooking the river valley and its wallpaper was scattered with little pink flowers.

Abbie looked at the west side of the room. "That would be the best place for a bed — you could wake up and see the river," she said. She sat down there and leaned against the wall, staring out at the glimpse of water below the screen of trees.

"This was Miss Kirkpatrick's room," decided Abbie. "This was where her bed was and this was where she died."

Again, she was amazed not to feel afraid. The realization only made her more courageous. She began to wonder what the old woman had been like. She recalled the tiny figure she had sometimes seen in the yard. Miss Kirkpatrick had always worn an apron, the kind with a bib, and black, laced shoes that seemed too large for her spindly legs. Her white hair was never combed and her expression was permanently bitter.

Yet, as Abbie remembered her, Miss Kirkpatrick only seemed lonely, not frightening. Of *course* she hadn't been a witch! She was just a sad old woman with no family or friends. Abbie wasn't sure how she knew all this so clearly — it was almost as if someone were whispering it in her mind.

She stretched out her legs in a patch of sunlight and made herself feel at home. Of course she shouldn't be trespassing, but she didn't think Miss Kirkpatrick would have minded.

Bacon appeared at the doorway of the room, the fur on his back stiff with fear. He stared at a spot beside Abbie and growled. Abbie laughed nervously. "It's all right, Bacon! There's no one here but me!" She made him lie down beside her. Bacon stopped growling, but he didn't stop quivering. He sniffed the air suspiciously.

Abbie suddenly wondered what time it was. She was supposed to be home for lunch, but she hated to leave. It was as if the house didn't want her to. Then she thought, I could come here every day! I have all of Easter break; a whole week when this house can be my secret.

She crept out silently, pushing Bacon ahead of her through the milk box. She ran out of the yard, then quietly walked home as if she were the same timid person of an hour ago.

For the rest of the week Abbie sneaked into the house every day. On the first few mornings she went immediately to the upstairs bedroom. She always sat in the same place by the side wall and gazed out the window, dreamily thinking about Miss Kirkpatrick. Abbie had no desire to move from that spot — it was like being under a spell.

She tried to imagine the old woman as a child, growing up here. Had she had brothers too? Had she been as lonely then as she was when she was old? Abbie remembered what her mother had said when Miss Kirkpatrick died: "What a pitiful existence — cooped up in that house all by herself. What a wasted life."

Usually Miss Kirkpatrick's room seemed warmer than the rest of the house — warm and welcoming. But sometimes Abbie sensed a heavy grief in the air, as if the old woman had suffered a great deal there.

On the third day everything changed. When Abbie entered Miss Kirkpatrick's bedroom, a strange sense of agitation took hold of her. She was filled with a certainty that there was something in the house she had to do, something she had to find.

She couldn't sit still. She started to inspect the rest of the house more thoroughly, poking into closets and even venturing into the musty basement. Her palms and knees got filthy and sore from crawling, but she couldn't seem to stop. It was as if someone were compelling her to search for something. Abbie knew the house had a hidden secret — Miss Kirkpatrick's secret. She went home that afternoon almost in tears because she hadn't discovered it.

That night she began to have disturbing dreams. She was searching and searching for something important while a gruff, desperate voice ordered, "Help me *find* it. Help me remember where I put it. . . ."

The next day Abbie stayed in the house for hours . All she could do was to repeat her search from the previous day, but she had no success. A few times she thought she heard a voice murmur in her ear, but she couldn't catch the words. Once she felt something, like the fabric of a sleeve, brush her arm.

"Is — is someone here?" Abbie whispered. The room was silent. "There's no one here but me," she told herself, but her voice shook with fear. If only the house were as peaceful as it had been when she'd first come! Now she wanted to run away from its demands, but she couldn't — not until she'd found Miss Kirkpatrick's secret.

She emerged from the house, dazed and blinking at the bright spring world. At home she was so silent and preoccupied that Mum asked her if she was sick.

Every night she heard the same pleading voice in her sleep. Every day she searched the house in vain, sometimes aware of a faint whisper or rustle. Someone else seemed to be looking alongside her, urging her on and not letting her rest.

On the sixth morning Abbie reached the house to find three people walking around in the backyard — a couple and a man dressed in work clothes.

"You'll need a new roof," the workman was saying. "And you'll want to get rid of a lot of these shrubs."

Abbie crouched in the back lane and pretended to tie her shoe. She listened while the man listed all the things that had to be done to the house. "We'll start tomorrow," he told the other two.

On shaking legs, Abbie walked home. She spent the rest of the day sitting in front of the television. Michael and Kyle were back from Jasper and bragged about their skiing stunts. Bacon brought her his ball to throw. But Abbie ignored them all and tried not to cry.

She could never visit the house again. She would never find whatever it was that Miss Kirkpatrick wanted her so much to find. She had tried her best, hadn't she? But she felt obliged to continue her search. Her head pounded with confusion. That evening she couldn't eat her dinner and Mum made her go to bed early, but Abbie couldn't sleep. She tossed under her hot blankets until she suddenly knew what she had to do. She had to go back to the house *that night*.

She tried to stay awake until everyone else had gone to bed, but in spite of herself she fell into a light, troubled sleep. "Help me find it, find it, find it . . ." pleaded the familiar voice.

"Find *what?*" asked Abbie desperately, and woke herself up. She remembered where she had to go. "I'm too scared," she whispered aloud, but she kept hearing the tragic voice from her dream.

Quickly she put on her darkest jeans and sweatshirt. She crept to her parents' bedroom: no sound. Bacon looked up sleepily from his basket in the hall, but Abbie shushed him and waved him back when he tried to follow her out the front door.

Outside it was dark and cold and windy. She pulled up the hood of her sweatshirt and ran to Miss Kirkpatrick's house as if she were running away from her fear. But she couldn't escape it; it filled her with dread as she forced herself in through the milk box.

At night the house did not seem friendly. Shadows flickered over the bare floors, the branch of a tree scraped against the window, and Abbie bumped into a low table that the workers must have left.

"Find it, find it," chanted the old woman's voice in

Abbie's head. Frantically she searched the whole house once more. An empty glass jar fell off a shelf and crashed on the basement floor. An upstairs door banged open and shut. By the time she reached the upstairs bedroom, Abbie was so frightened she thought she would throw up.

Inside the bedroom she moved through a patch of icy air. An invisible hand clutched her wrist for a second, then let go. Abbie collapsed on the floor in the same spot where she had sat for the first few days. "I can't find it!" she sobbed. "I'm s-sorry, I just *can't*. . . ." She was filled with a piercing grief, the grief of someone very close to her in the room.

After a few minutes Abbie lifted her wet face and stared out the window. It was hopeless; she'd never find it, and she could never come back. Miss Kirkpatrick's secret would be lost forever.

Suddenly the wind shifted the clouds and moonlight streamed into the room, making a path on the floor. Abbie's eyes followed it to the open closet, where she saw a crack in one of the walls. There was a panel there. Pushing back her hair, she got to her feet and stumbled into the closet. She tore at the crack with her fingernails. At first the panel was stuck, but then it came loose easily, as if someone else were helping pull. Putting her hand in the space behind the panel, Abbie felt around, then jerked back. Her hand was covered in furry, damp dust. What horrible thing was in there?

"*Find it*," a voice said aloud. Abbie forced herself to reach in again and feel around at the bottom of the cavity. Her hand closed on something long and smooth. She pulled it out and took it to the window. Her body trembled as she sat down to examine her find in the moonlight.

It was a thick roll of papers, tied up with a frayed green ribbon. Abbie blew off the dust, unrolled the papers, and stared. The pages were covered with delicate drawings and watercolor paintings of cups, chairs, pine needles, mountain ash berries, and lilac flowers. Each object looked as if you could pluck it off the page and hold it in your hand.

Abbie squinted at the pictures in the dim light. One showed the remains of a sandwich on a blue-patterned plate, every crumb carefully outlined with a fine brush. In another a bouquet of wild roses sat in a chipped glass, the water barely suggested in skillful strokes. A third showed the view from the upstairs bedroom in winter, with the blue shadows of the snow contrasting with the gray expanse of the frozen river.

The last drawing was of a face. Abbie lingered over it. A thin, plain young woman stared back at her, her expression serious and intense. At the bottom of the page was a long-ago date and a signature in faded brown ink — Catherine Kirkpatrick.

Catherine. So that was her name. Warm air caressed

Abbie and she knew Catherine was pleased with her for finding her secret.

She could never come back to Catherine's house, but now she had these wonderful pictures. She could take them home and look at them whenever she wanted. She would have a part of Catherine forever.

But when she rolled up the papers, the room grew cold again. As she walked downstairs a force of heavy air pushed against her chest. She tripped at the entrance to the kitchen, and when she bent to open the door of the milk box, the familiar gruff voice ordered, "Leave them!"

Abbie twisted the sheaf of pictures around and around in her hands. "All right." She sighed. "I understand." Reluctantly she laid them on the workmen's table, worried that they might just throw them out. But as she turned to go, the warm air surrounded her again and she knew that Catherine approved.

Abbie crawled through the milk box and ran home. Silently she slipped into the house and climbed upstairs to her bed, where she sank into a dreamless sleep.

"Did you hear about what they discovered in the Kirkpatrick house?" Abbie's father said at dinner a few days later. "A lot of drawings and paintings that the old lady had done. Apparently they're incredibly good. They're going to frame them and exhibit them at the art gallery. The house's new owners have generously donated them."

"So Miss Kirkpatrick was a secret artist!" exclaimed Abbie's mother. "What a surprise!"

"What's most surprising is that they didn't find the pictures earlier, when they were moving out the furniture," said Dad. "Apparently they just appeared, as if someone had put them there."

"Wow . . . spooky. Eh, Abbie?" teased Kyle.

He looked surprised when Abbie just grinned at him. But she still had one more thing to find out.

By fall the old house had become the pride of the neighborhood. The new owners had painted the shutters blue and the door bright red. They had clipped the lawn and trimmed the overgrown shrubs. One evening Abbie's parents were asked over for coffee. Abbie begged to go with them.

Inside Miss Kirkpatrick's house she looked around intently at the gleaming paint and soft furniture as the two couples chatted.

"May I use the bathroom?" she asked. She didn't add that she already knew where it was. She crept upstairs with a beating heart, and went straight to Catherine's room. The new owners had put their bed in exactly the right place, on the west side of the room with a view of the river.

Abbie stood there for a long time. Nothing. The air was free of loneliness and grief. Catherine had gone.

• • •

Maria Leach

THE GHOSTLY SPOOLS

Years ago in old French Canada, in the time when people were still spinning yarn to make their homespun garments, an old grandmother of the village used to hire women of the neighborhood to come to her house to spin and wind the yarn on spools.

One day one of the poor old women stole some of the spools, and very shortly after that she sickened and died.

Soon after the funeral the old grandmother woke up in the night and heard a noise in the attic over her bedroom. It sounded like wooden spools rolling around on the attic floor. "I'll go look in the morning," she said to herself.

In the morning she went up to the attic to look around, but she could not see or find anything unusual.

She heard the noise again the next night. It sounded exactly like wooden spools rolling and clattering around on the attic floor. She searched the attic again but found nothing. Every night after that the sound of spools rolling around would wake her up and keep her awake.

Then one night, in the middle of the night, when she heard the spools rolling, she suddenly remembered the poor old neighbor who had stolen some of her spools.

"It must be Lucie," she thought. (That was the old neighbor's name.) "She's bringing them back!"

Quickly she got out of bed and went up the attic stairs; softly she opened the attic door at the top of the stairs; softly she called: "Lucie, Lucie! Is that you? It's all right, Lucie," she said. "You can have the spools."

At once the sound stopped, and the old grandmother never heard it again.

• • •

THE GIRL IN THE ROSE-COLORED SHAWL

Elsie saw her first. "Isn't that a little girl up ahead? See, she has a rose-colored shawl around her. She can't be more than eight or nine years old. Is anyone with her?"

"What is she doing alone in these hills?" Willis asked. "There isn't a house for miles."

It was a vivid spring day when the grass was its brightest green and the water in the river shimmered in the sun. Wildflowers were blooming in the nearby woods and dandelions filled the ditches.

Willis slowed the car as they neared the spot where the child stood gazing at them. Pale gold curly hair framed a pinched triangular face and her gray eyes were steady. With one hand she was clutching the shawl close around her against the spring breeze; with the other she held a bouquet of wildflowers. Willis braked to a stop as Elsie rolled down the window.

"Can we give you a ride, dear? You must have walked

a long way for those flowers."

The child looked down at her dusty boots and then at the car.

"Here, let me open that door for you." Willis went around to the other side of the car to help her.

"I'm sure your mother has told you not to ride with strangers," he said gently, "but we can't leave you alone way out here. It will be dark before long."

The little girl clambered up onto the wide back seat with her flowers, and sat stiffly as the door was closed beside her.

Elsie asked, "What is your name, dear?"

"Annie," she whispered.

"Well, Annie, let us know when we come to your house."

Willis broke the silence of the ride once or twice with comments about the beauty of the day or the sight of a high-flying eagle. But the little girl responded only to Elsie.

"Where is your house?" Elsie asked.

"Up 'tar."

"Were you out walking by yourself?"

"Ess."

"Are those flowers hepaticas?"

"Ess."

"What color is your house?"

"White house round t' bend."

Elsie concentrated on watching for a white house. On and on Willis drove, rounding bend after bend. But the shadows were long before they finally saw a roof top ahead. The place appeared to be old and abandoned.

"This can't be your house, Annie," said Willis as they drew up before the sagging building. The windows had been boarded over and the veranda was falling off. There was no sign of life anywhere. It was hard to say if the house had ever been white, as there was not a fleck of paint left on the old boards.

Elsie turned to ask again if they had the right place. THE BACK SEAT WAS EMPTY.

"*Willis, she's gone!*"

"She can't be. The door never opened!"

"Turn the car, Willis. Maybe she fell out."

"Don't be ridiculous," he said. "I tell you, the door never opened." But he wheeled around in the overgrown driveway and headed back the way they had come.

They traveled as far as the place where they had picked up the child. Until complete darkness settled over the hills, Willis and Elsie drove back and forth, back and forth along that road. They peered into the woods, up the green slopes, and across the river, trying to penetrate the deepening shadows.

But there was no little girl in a rose-colored shawl.

• • •

Ken Roberts

THE CLOSET

The house had been constructed to look old, with gables and porches and rounded windows. A swimming pool was being built at one side. Uncle Gus stood on the porch, waiting. He was a big man, bald on top but with long dark hair running down each side of his head. He watched the car stop and then quickly walked down the steps, his arms open wide.

Uncle Gus threw his arms around Jeremy's dad as he stepped out of the car. Jeremy turned to look. Uncle Gus was staring at him over his father's shoulder.

"You must be Jeremy," he said, smiling. "Don't just sit there, kid. Hop out so I can see you."

Jeremy unfastened his seat belt and crawled out. Uncle Gus ran around the car and grabbed him by the shoulders. "How old are you Jeremy? Nine?"

"Twelve," said Jeremy.

Uncle Gus shrugged. "I don't have any kids, so I don't

29

know. I've never needed kids. I'm my own kid. Come inside and see the house. You're going to like this place. It's got some weird things in it, but where's the harm, eh? If it feels right, do it. That's what I say."

Uncle Gus ran ahead and held open the front door.

Just inside the wide entrance hall sat two amusement park bumper cars, one red and the other green. The cars were polished and bright. Their seats were covered in soft brown leather. Each car had a metal pole mounted behind the driver's seat. The poles reached toward the dark, metal ceiling. The hall was lined with black rubber baseboards made from tires sliced in half.

"I turned on the power," said Uncle Gus with a grin.

"These don't actually work, do they, Gus?" asked Jeremy's dad.

"Sure." Uncle Gus laughed. "Not in the whole house, of course. They work in the hall and in the library. Where's the harm, eh? It felt right, so I did it. Try one, Jeremy."

Jeremy glanced at his father. "Why not?" said Dad.

Jeremy sat down in the red car, running his hands over the steering wheel. He pressed the pedal and sped down the hallway, turning into the library. The room was filled with bookcases, floor to ceiling and wall to wall. The hardwood floor was bare, except for a comfortable chair and a lamp that stood on a raised island. The island and the bookcases were surrounded by rubber bumpers.

"Wow!" Jeremy exclaimed. He looked back. His dad and Uncle Gus were standing by the door. Uncle Gus reached toward the nearest bookcase and pulled on a book. It tipped forward and fell open. The book was hollow. Buttons blinked inside the cover.

"Watch that wall," said Uncle Gus, pointing toward the far side of the room. "You'll like this, Jeremy. Every home should have one."

Uncle Gus pushed some buttons.

The lights dimmed. Flashes of simulated lightning lit a big bay window. Slow organ music boomed into the room. A spookhouse laugh, loud and threatening, echoed from behind the ceiling. The far wall began to move, rolling back into a hidden recess.

"Great sound system, eh?" shouted Uncle Gus.

Behind the far bookcase was a wooden door. The door slowly creaked open to reveal a closet. Old clothes hung limply from hangers, and a shelf above the clothes was stacked with worn-out leather suitcases and cardboard boxes. Everything was coated with fake spider webs. An antique wooden trunk sat on the closet floor. Slowly the trunk's lid began to open. A human skull appeared over the rim.

Small yellow lights in the eye sockets made the skull seem as though it was peering at the three people in the room. One by one, bony fingers gripped the edge of the trunk. Then, leaning on both hands, an entire skeleton

31

rose from within. It stepped out of the trunk, and a spotlight shot across the room to light it. The sound-track laughter stopped, replaced a moment later by fast-paced ragtime music. The skeleton began to dance like a reluctant marionette.

When the music stopped, the skeleton stepped back into the trunk and collapsed. The lid slammed shut and the closet door slowly closed. The bookcase slid into place and Uncle Gus turned on the library lights.

"You know the old saying," he said as he tilted the hollow book back into the wall. "Everyone's got a skeleton in the closet. Well, I decided this house needed a real skeleton in a real closet. Where's the harm, eh? It felt right, so I did it."

"That's not a real skeleton, though," said Jeremy uneasily. "It's made of plastic, right?"

"No, it's real," said Uncle Gus. "Why buy something fake when you can get the real thing?"

"You bought a skeleton?" Jeremy whispered.

"Kids are so morbid," said Uncle Gus, grinning. "My neighbor is a doctor, Jeremy. He got the skeleton for me from a medical supplies catalog. Where's the harm, eh? It felt right, so I did it. I'm not buying one for you, though."

Uncle Gus pointed at his nephew and squinted down his finger as if he were aiming a pistol. "Not without your dad's permission," he added with a wink.

Jeremy's father didn't say anything.

Uncle Gus ran out of the room. A moment later Jeremy heard a bumper car speed down the hall. "Try to catch me!" Uncle Gus yelled.

Jeremy tried, but he didn't try hard.

After dinner Uncle Gus showed them the billiards room. "There's lot of neat stuff all over this house," he said to Jeremy. "You explore while we play a couple of games. Have fun, kid."

Jeremy stood by the door for a few minutes and then walked across the hall to the library. It was dark. He fumbled with the books by the door until he found the one that leaned forward. There were two buttons inside the book, one red and one green.

Jeremy pushed the green button. The far wall silently began to roll back. Jeremy figured the red button was for the music. He didn't push it. He walked across the room and waited.

The closet door swung open and the trunk lid rose. The skull lifted its head.

"Who are you?" Jeremy whispered, standing in front of the trunk. He could see wires connecting the skeleton to the ceiling.

The skeleton stepped out of the trunk and began to jiggle, its bones rattling against each other. The dance finished, and the skeleton stepped back into the trunk and lay down. The lid closed.

Jeremy stepped into the closet and lifted the lid. "Who are you?" he asked again.

The closet door slammed shut. The bookcase began to roll. Quickly Jeremy twisted the closet door handle. It opened, and he leaped back into the library.

"Who are you?" he asked once more.

From behind the bookcase Jeremy was almost sure he heard a voice whisper, "Help me."

Gus escorted his guests to the top of the stairs and said goodnight. Jeremy carried his suitcase into his room. He heard a noise behind him and whirled around.

"I came to say goodnight," said his dad.

Jeremy relaxed. "Goodnight," he said.

"You've been awfully quiet tonight, Jeremy."

"I've just been thinking."

"Try to sleep. We'll leave in the morning."

"Do you like Uncle Gus, Dad?"

"He's my older brother, Jeremy. We grew up together."

"But do you like him, Dad?"

"Jeremy, I haven't seen Gus for years. If he hadn't moved here, halfway to your grandmother's house, I probably wouldn't have seen him for another few years. I guess I like him. I want to like him."

"How did Uncle Gus get rich?"

"He writes video games. Gus always liked games. Mom used to worry. 'He's such a daydreamer,' she'd say. He grew up and became a professional daydreamer. Good for him."

"Dad?"

"Yeah?"

"That skeleton . . ."

"I know, Jeremy. There's a real person in that closet, right? What can we do, though?"

"We could . . ."

"We can't do anything," said Dad firmly, "except to leave in the morning. Get some sleep. Nothing else will happen."

But Jeremy's dad was wrong.

Jeremy didn't know what woke him or what made him look toward the door. First the doorway was empty and then, a moment later, a ghost stood looking toward his bed. It was tall and round, a white cloud with pale eyes and a colorless mouth. The mouth began to move.

"Bury me," the ghost whispered.

Jeremy knew at once that the ghost belonged to his uncle's skeleton. He shivered.

"Bury me," the ghost said again.

Jeremy breathed deeply and stood up. The skeleton

drifted to one side of the doorway, making room for Jeremy to pass.

When Jeremy reached the library, the closet was open. The skeleton was dancing, and its eyes flashed. Jeremy ran to the closet and yanked at the wires. Nothing happened. Each wire was hooked to the skeleton with a clasp. Nervously, Jeremy fiddled with one clasp until at last a bony leg sprung loose.

Jeremy disconnected all the clasps until the skeleton fell into his arms. He gasped, terrified that the skeleton would move, but it lay still. Jeremy hauled it out of the closet and laid it on the hardwood floor. He looked toward the library door. The cloud was standing there, waiting. "Bury me," it whispered.

His heart pounding fast, Jeremy carried the skeleton out the front door of his uncle's house.

"Bury me," the ghost whispered from somewhere nearby.

Jeremy began to disassemble the bones. "I'm not burying you with any bolts attached."

When he was finished, Jeremy took off his pajama top and tied the bones inside. He gently carried the shirt across the lawn to where the swimming pool was being constructed. He found a shovel and began to dig where the concrete deck would be poured. "They'll never find you here," he muttered.

Suddenly Jeremy heard a noise behind him. He spun around. His father was standing three meters away.

"What are you doing out here in your pajamas? Where's your top? What the heck's going on?"

"I'm burying the skeleton, Dad. I saw it."

"We all saw it, but that doesn't mean you can steal . . ."

"No, Dad. I saw the ghost of the skeleton."

"No, you didn't, Jeremy," said Dad slowly. "There is no such thing as a ghost. You're a daydreamer, Jeremy. Just like your uncle Gus."

"I'm not anything like Uncle Gus!"

"Well, you've sure got his imagination."

"Ghost!" shouted Jeremy. "If you want your skeleton to get buried, you'd better say something."

A breeze gently rocked the trees. An owl hooted.

"Bury me," whispered the ghost. "Bury me."

"It's some kind of trick," said Jeremy's dad. "Uncle Gus is playing a joke."

"No, he isn't."

"Bury me," said the ghost.

"There, Dad! In the pool!"

Jeremy's father looked down into the pool. The cloud floated in a dark corner.

Jeremy lifted his pajama top. "I took the skeleton apart, Dad, and I can't put it back together. It's too late."

Jeremy's father stared at the bag of bones. "Give me

the shovel," he mumbled at last. "Quickly! Before I change my mind."

When they were finished, Jeremy and his father stared down at the small grave. "Rest in peace," said Dad softly.

Together they walked slowly toward the house.

Uncle Gus was standing at the open door, silhouetted by the hallway lights. "I heard talking and got up," he said. "I've been to the library. I want my skeleton back."

It was the first time Jeremy had heard Uncle Gus finish a sentence without adding a laugh.

"We buried the skeleton," he said calmly.

"But why?" asked Uncle Gus.

"I guess," said Jeremy's dad, "it just felt like the right thing to do, Gus."

"So we did it," added Jeremy. "It felt right, so we did it."

• • •

Karleen Bradford

WHO'S INVISIBLE NOW?

"Don't sit on Eleanor!" Jane screamed.

Her mother's best friend, Mrs. Tripp, leaped back up from the chair upon which she was about to sit, and spilled her tea. She looked at Jane's mother and raised one eyebrow.

"Eleanor's still with us, I see," she said, mopping at the spilled tea on her lap with her handkerchief.

"Really, Jane, this business of your invisible friend is becoming a nuisance," Mrs. Lister said, running for the paper towels.

"I'm sorry, Mrs. Tripp," Jane said. "She was just sitting there for a minute, waiting for me to come so we could go up to my room."

"Er . . . Jane, dear," Mrs. Tripp said, looking at her over the tops of her huge, black-rimmed glasses. "Don't you think you'd be happier with a *real* friend? My Susie would love to see more of you, I know."

Jane muttered something that tried to sound polite and ran from the room.

Later on, when Mrs. Lister had come in to turn Jane's light off for the night for the third time, she looked down at Jane and sighed.

"Mrs. Tripp is right, you know, dear. You are really much too old to have an imaginary friend. That's what little children do, and you're nearly eleven. Why don't you try to forget about Eleanor and play more with Susie — she's such a delightful, well-adjusted child."

"Eleanor is not imaginary," Jane replied sulkily. "She's just invisible, that's all. And you're always telling me to be loyal to my friends, so why shouldn't that include Eleanor? Anyway, Susie's not a 'delightful, well-adjusted child.' She's a fink."

"Really, dear! That word!"

"It's not a bad word. It's in the dictionary. I looked it up the last time you told me not to say it. If it's all right for the dictionary, it should be all right for me and it sure describes Susie. 'Fink: Spy; informer. Unsavory person; jerk.' That's Susie."

"Jane! Susie's certainly not a spy."

"Oh, yes she is. She's the one who told the whole class about Eleanor, after you told her mother. She eavesdropped when you two were talking and then she told the whole world. That's a spy. And she's a jerk because Eleanor said so."

"Oh, dear." Mrs. Lister sighed and left the room, forgetting to turn the light out after all.

Jane sighed too, and turned the light off herself. She didn't really mind people not believing in Eleanor — after all, she couldn't expect them to — but it did make things difficult sometimes.

The next morning, as she was coming down the stairs to breakfast, she heard her mother and father talking. She didn't mean to eavesdrop — *she* wasn't a spy — but she couldn't help overhearing the tail end of their conversation.

"I don't know what to do about this Eleanor business, I really don't," her mother was saying.

"Maybe if we got her busy doing other things," her father replied. "Maybe that would take her mind off Eleanor for a while."

The next week was school break, and Jane was certainly kept busy. Her mother stayed home from work and had something different planned for every day of the week: movies one day, puppet show the next, shopping for shoes the next, visit to Susie's house (ugh) the next. They even went to the zoo. Jane had a marvelous time.

The evening before school started again her mother and father called her back into the living room just as she was going to bed.

"Did you enjoy yourself over the holiday?" her father

asked. They were both looking at her expectantly.

"Oh, I certainly did," Jane answered, her eyes shining. "And so did Eleanor. Every minute of it, except for the visit to Susie's." She bounced out of the room.

Mrs. Lister gave a little shriek of despair.

"I give up," Mr. Lister said, and retreated into his newspaper.

The next day after school Jane's mother was waiting for her with a batch of freshly baked chocolate chip-oatmeal cookies. Her favorite kind.

"Load up," Mrs. Lister said, her voice unusually stern. "We're going to take a walk."

They walked until dinner. Jane's mother explained patiently why almost-eleven-year-old girls shouldn't have imaginary — "I mean invisible," she corrected herself quickly — playmates. They admired their neighbors' lawns and gardens, stopped in for an ice-cream cone — very unusual this, so close to dinner time and after all those cookies too, thought Jane — talked about school, then started back home. Mrs. Lister began to explain all over again about invisible playmates and almost-eleven-year-old girls, but Jane suddenly interrupted her.

"Just a moment, Mom," she said politely. "Eleanor thinks her mother's calling her."

"Eleanor!" exploded Mrs. Lister. "What have I just been telling you? ELEANOR DOESN'T EXIST!"

Just then, out of the thin air and only a child's-breath away from Jane, a mother's impatient voice cried out: "Really, Eleanor, this business of your invisible friend Jane is becoming a nuisance. I've called you three times for dinner now. Will you *please* come in!"

• • •

Dennis Lee

THERE WAS A MAN

There was a man who never was.
This tragedy occurred because
His parents, being none too smart,
Were born two hundred years apart.

Janet Lunn

WEBSTER'S ROOF

Dear Hilary,

I know this is only my second time writing to you, and our teacher said not to tell our pen pals our entire life story in the first couple of letters, but I have to tell you this or I'll burst. Everybody says England is full of ghosts and stuff like that, so I'm hoping you won't laugh or think I'm nuts.

This thing happened last weekend, when my mother got her usual case of spring-planting disease. She reorganizes the whole backyard every year. She moves all the flower beds. She even moves the bushes.

So there we were in the backyard, all ten meters square of it, and General Pershing was in command. (Our name — Pershing — is the same as some famous American general, so when she's bossing us around, like at spring-planting time, we all call my mother General Pershing.)

This was just the kind of day she likes best. There

was lots of sun, hardly any clouds, and a bright blue sky. The smell of lilacs was absolutely everywhere. It wasn't the kind of day for spooky things to happen at all.

The general was standing on the patio with boxes and boxes of flowers, and she had on her horrible old straw hat and her baggy orange pants. My brother, Michael (he's five), was over in his corner of the yard building roads. I guess I'd better tell you about Michael's roads, because they're a big part of this thing that happened.

Michael has been making roads in our backyard since before he could walk. They're over by our neighbor's big willow tree and they go everywhere — through tiny towns, up hills, through tunnels, in cloverleafs like real highways. In the towns he's got street lights made out of those little square paintbox colors and along the highways there are telephone poles made out of popsicle sticks connected with wires that used to be Dad's guitar strings.

You can just bet there are some humongous battles over those roads. Last year my mother drew a line with her trowel where she said they had to stop. It's kind of like a moat, and Michael isn't allowed to make even one dead-end road outside that moat.

We were all working so hard that all you could hear were the cars and lawnmowers up the street, the birds chattering in the lilac bush and the willow tree, and our trowels scraping stones. The general was in full swing:

"Katie, bring me that flat of lavender, and don't step on my bougainvillaea.

"David [that's my father], you're going to have to help me dig this hole for the new cypress tree. I can't imagine why it's so tough."

"Don't dig there. That's Webster's roof." Suddenly there was so much silence in the backyard you could almost hear it. I swear even the birds stopped singing. Michael was standing right beside Mom.

He said it again. "Don't dig there. It's Webster's roof."

The general put down her shovel. "Michael, what are you talking about?"

"Webster. He lives there, under his roof."

"Michael, who is Webster?" You could tell she was getting impatient by the way she pushed back her hat.

"He's just Webster, and he lives there." Michael was getting impatient too. You could tell because he was doing the same thing to his hat.

Mom smiled her teacher's smile. (When she's not ordering us around, my mother orders grade fivers around in our school.) "Now, Mikey," she said, "there's no one living under our backyard. Brownies and elves and fairies live in Britain and France and other countries way across the ocean. They don't live in suburban backyards here in Canada. Really they don't."

Michael didn't look at all convinced, but Mom had another idea. "You know, Mikey, I think Webster will like

47

having our beautiful new tree growing out of his house."
She was trying to humor him. My mother should have
known better than that.

"He'll hate it. Don't dig there."

My dad is a pacifist. He marched right into the war
zone, grabbed Michael, sat him up on his shoulders, and
rode him out of the backyard, singing, "Ice cream time,
oh jolly ice cream time," to the tune of *Alouette* as he
went. Michael tried to grab the backyard gate, but he
couldn't reach that far down from Dad's shoulders. He
kept shouting, "Don't dig up Webster's roof! Don't dig up
Webster's roof," all the way to the car.

But of course, Mom did — or, rather, we both did. I
had to cut a neat circle with the shovel, and together the
general and I sliced the grass off. It looked like a pot lid
without the knob on top. Actually, I shouldn't say we
sliced it — it was so tough, we yanked and shoved as
much as we sliced. Honestly, the stuff we pulled out of
there was weird! It was gray and ropy and gummy, and it
had bits of bark and sticks stuck to it. It made me feel
funny after what Michael said.

Dad and Michael got back with the ice cream before
we could dig the hole. And then we had lunch.

Right after lunch we were back there. Only, the hole
was gone. The lid was back on it. My mother was really
teed off. "Michael," she said in that slow, low voice that
makes you want to jump right out of your skin. Michael

jumped. He didn't exactly look guilty, but he sure looked uncomfortable.

"I didn't put it back," he said. "Probably Webster did. I told you not to dig there." Michael's face was redder than the geraniums Mom was going to put along the back fence. And his shoulders were hunched right up to his ears.

"Well, *you* can just take that round of sod off that hole, because I want to plant my tree there."

Michael didn't budge.

"Get busy, young man." The general was losing it.

"I won't." Michael didn't look at her, but he wasn't moving as much as his little toe.

"Michael!" The general sounded dangerous. Dad came down from the patio.

"You know, Ginny," he said (that's the general's first name), "I wonder if this *is* the best spot for your cypress tree. In two or three years it might start crowding out the lilac bush. Cypresses grow to be quite a size."

Mother looked at Dad. She looked at the tree. Then she looked at Michael. You could see she wasn't hot to give up the fight. She looked at the tree again.

"You're perfectly right." She went over and stood beside Dad and squinted at the lilac bush and then at the hole. "I think maybe it would be better up near the patio. It will throw a great shadow in the evening when it's full grown. But moving the tree is no reason to give in to a child's fantasies. I think I'll plant an azalea in that hole.

Now, Michael, will you please take up that round of sod."

Michael got redder and redder. His shoulders were moving up past his ears, but he wasn't giving in. My mother wasn't giving in either, and being the mother, she had the upper hand. She sent Michael to his room and made me pull up the chunk of grass and all that gray ropy stuff. It really gave me the creeps when it was just as hard to pull out the second time.

We got it all out. Underneath it was all hollow, as if something really did live there. I was glad we had to go to the plant nursery to buy the azalea. We didn't get back to the hole until the next day.

Mom had made Michael promise not to go near the azalea bush hole. Someone did. The next morning the hole was gone again, and this time I don't just mean the lid was back on. I mean there wasn't any hole. You couldn't even see the line where the shovel had cut into the grass.

I went over and sat beside Michael. He was fixing up a bridge. "How did you get it so perfect?" I asked him.

"Webster messed up my bridge." Michael wasn't crying, but his eyes looked so sad. One of the little plastic bridges was over on its side. "He knocked over all the supports. See where his stick poked holes in the ground? And I never touched his old roof." Michael went back to fixing up the bridge.

When Mom came out and saw there wasn't any hole,

she hit the roof — she hit Webster's roof, that's for sure. I bet you can tell that, by this time, I was almost believing there was a Webster. I mean, how could Michael put back that grass lid so you couldn't even see the shovel marks? And who made all those tiny little holes around Michael's bridge? But the general didn't stop to think about that. She was too mad. She just made me dig the hole up all over again and wouldn't even let Michael tell her about his bridge. She shook her finger at him, and said, "Don't bother me over some neighborhood dog rooting up your roads for a place to bury his bone."

When we finally got all that stuff out of there and filled the hollow place with top soil and got the azalea in, I was awfully glad it was finished. I had this feeling all the time I was working that someone was watching me. It wasn't Michael. I know because I kept looking up to see and he never looked at us once. He didn't make any more roads. He just sat there sort of like he was guarding them. Maybe Mom felt funny, too, because she didn't scold Michael again. She just said, "I think we'd better finish that ice cream we bought yesterday. Come on."

But Michael wouldn't come inside for ice cream. When Mom went out of the kitchen, I scooped another scoop into my cone and took it out to him. I didn't blame him for wanting to watch his roads after what happened.

Isn't this weird? I mean, when you read all this, do you think there could be something named Webster living under our backyard in Scarborough, Ontario, Canada? Well, believe it or not, there's more to the Michael/Mom/Webster business. Dad had to carry Michael in for supper. Michael yelled and screamed that he was going to stay outside all night. Michael never yells and screams. Then he wouldn't eat any supper. Michael never doesn't eat any supper. Finally he went all quiet, not mad or soreheaded, just quiet. I felt awful.

After Michael was put to bed, and Mom and Dad went back downstairs to the living room, I went in to see him. He was standing at the window, looking out at the backyard. The patio light was on, so the rest of the yard was dark. You couldn't see the roads, or the azalea plant, or even the lilac bush. You could only see the new cypress tree with its little pointy shadow that was going to be so big and wonderful some day.

"Do you want me to go out and look after your roads?" I asked him. I really would have stayed outside all night myself, if only to make Michael stop looking as if the whole world was going to end before morning.

"It doesn't matter." He kicked the wall under the window. "She won't leave his roof alone and Webster's going to be so mad he'll ruin all my roads. I know he will."

"Won't he know you didn't dig up his roof?"

"I guess he won't."

Michael didn't make any noise. Tears just started pouring down his face. I couldn't stand it. I gave him a hug, then sneaked downstairs and out the back door. I wanted to pull out the stupid azalea, but I didn't dare. I sort of wished Webster would show up, so I could tell him it wasn't Michael's fault. Then I got so scared there might really be a Webster that I ran back into the house and went right to bed.

The next morning Michael was white as a corpse and he didn't want any breakfast. Before Mom and Dad could get after him to eat, I went out to see if his roads were OK.

You guessed it. They weren't. You've never seen anything like that mess. His roads looked as if three hurricanes and a couple of tornadoes had hit them. You almost couldn't see where they used to be. The telephone poles were down, the wires were broken, the paintbox lights were all over the place. Bridges and tunnels were smashed, the roads looked as if somebody had kicked them, and there were those little holes all over the place. I was so mad I shouted, "Webster, you're a skunk!" Then I ran into the house and grabbed my mother's arm before she could reach for her coffee cup.

"Come on." I felt like the general now. "Come outside and look." She came.

"Look at it," I said. "Disaster city and it's all your fault. Webster's so mad about his roof, he's paying Michael back. But it's not Michael's fault, it's yours! Don't you care?"

My mother didn't say a word. She looked at the mess, then looked at her azalea. It was still there, but it was a little lopsided now. Her mouth was open and her eyes were bugging out. Finally she said, "Katie, what do you think has happened?" So I told her. I told her I thought there really was a Webster — whoever he was, whatever he was — living where Michael said he lived and that he — Webster, I mean — didn't want anybody messing up his house.

My mother is bossy, but she isn't mean. I don't think she really believed me about Webster, but she believed how terrible Michael felt about his roads and she was really surprised at me for shouting at her. (You don't shout at General Pershing.) She looked at the disaster area again, and shook her head as if she couldn't believe it.

"I'll tell you what, Michael," she said back in the kitchen, after she'd sat down and swallowed a couple of big gulps of coffee. "When we get home from school this afternoon, we'll make a new hole for the azalea."

"OK," said Michael. And I guess it was OK, because he started eating his breakfast.

Well, that's still not the end. That afternoon, before the general had even had a cup of tea, she and I went outside and dug a new hole for the azalea plant. It was easy. Then we took out all the topsoil and put back all the stuff from the old hole and put the grass lid on top.

Mom gave it a good pat. After she went into the house, I gave it another pat. "OK, Webster?" I asked.

Before I went to bed that night, I went outside again. The moon was full, so the yard was very bright. The lilac bush and the big willow tree and the little new cypress made black shadows on the grass and there was just enough wind to rustle the leaves. It gave me the shivers, and it was easy to believe that there could be a Webster living in our backyard in Scarborough, Ontario, Canada.

I looked at the old azalea-cypress tree hole and it looked the same as when we first finished putting the lid back on. I went over and stood in front of it. Some of the gray ropy stuff was leaking out of the edges. "Webster," I said, "you won. You won hands down. So what about it?"

I stamped around the backyard a little to show Webster I wasn't scared of him, then I went inside.

First thing the next morning Michael came racing inside from the backyard. Mom was just coming down the stairs. "Guess what?" he said. "Webster's fixed up my roads. He didn't do them exactly right, but that's OK. I can do the rest."

I dropped the box of cornflakes I was holding and ran out to look. Mom and Dad were right behind me. It was true. The roads were back. It was true, too, that they weren't perfect. The bridges were lumpy and the tunnels weren't big enough for the cars and I don't think Webster understands what telephone poles are for because they were set up down the middle of all the roads. But as Michael said, he could fix those things up.

So that's about it. It wasn't really ghosts, I guess — in fact, I don't know what it was . . . or is. What do you think?

Your Pen Pal,
Katie Pershing

• • •

Sharon Siamon

STAIRS

When I was twelve, we lived in a spooky old house on Clinton Street in Toronto. My mother and I and her friend Wanda lived there for ten months while Mom went back to school. Wanda was an art student. She helped pay the rent and stayed with me when Mom had night classes at the university.

Number 83 Clinton was a dump. Mom said all that held it together were the layers of old paint and wallpaper on the walls. The whole house seemed to creak and moan when you climbed the stairs.

There were a lot of stairs in that Clinton house: the dark stairway to our apartment on the second floor; a narrow, steep set of stairs to Wanda's attic room; and twenty-seven stairs from our back door off the kitchen to the ground outside. That outdoor staircase was pretty rickety. We used it mostly for letting our cat, Toby, in and out.

One night Toby disappeared. You know how cats can get spooked and make dashes at things that aren't there? Sometimes they're playing, chasing an imaginary mouse; but sometimes they run like fury, as if something is after them. That's how Toby was the day she ran away. She dashed down the hall from the bedroom and hid under the kitchen table. She begged to go out, but when we let her, she sat on the windowsill and stared back at us through the glass. It was as if she could see something fearful in the kitchen. And then that night she didn't come in when we called. We felt terrible. Mom and I had had Toby ever since we lived out west. She'd come across the country with us in our old Chev, which was full of all our stuff. Wanda said the ghost had scared our cat away.

Wanda had recently started a series of cat drawings, and had tacked them up in the hall that ran down one side of our apartment. The morning after Toby disappeared, some of them were torn off the wall.

"I know you're unhappy about losing your cat," Wanda told me as she put them back up, "but you didn't have to rip my drawings down."

"I didn't! I wouldn't!" I really liked Wanda and her pictures, and I was sad about Toby. I started to cry.

Wanda gave me a hug. "I'm sorry, Karen. But who could have done it? Your mom?"

"Not Mom." I stared at her. "She's crazy about your pictures."

"Well, then." Wanda threw up her arms and all her wrist bangles jingled. She started down the hall. "It must be the ghost."

"Ghost?" I wasn't sure what I'd heard. "What ghost?" I ran after Wanda. That long, narrow hall was like a funhouse at the fair. I had to reach out with one arm to keep my balance on the sloping floor. The floor was so slanted that if you dropped a ball, it would roll over to one side and back toward the kitchen. "What ghost?" I demanded again, grabbing Wanda's arm.

She was already pouring herself a cup of herbal tea at the kitchen counter. Her long dark hair swung forward over her face. "I hear it when I'm working at night," she said casually. She flipped her hair back and turned to face me. The light caught the crystal she wore round her neck and shot rainbows around the kitchen. "Don't worry, I think it's a friendly ghost. It just goes up and down the stairs, very slowly, one step at a time. Sometimes I hear it singing."

"Are you making this up?" I gasped. I perched on the kitchen table where I could stare at her eyeball to eyeball.

"No, I'm not." Wanda sipped her tea and leaned against the sink. "It sings funny old songs. I just catch snatches of the words. . . . I think that's why Toby left," she added. "Cats are very sensitive."

I shivered, remembering the wild look in Toby's eyes. What had frightened her?

"I think the ghost tripped over Toby one night," Wanda went on. "I heard it shout, 'Get out of my way, or I'll kick your tail from here to tomorrow!' Of course, ghosts don't trip, they just walk right through things." Wanda shoved her hair behind her ears and rattled her dangling earrings. "I guess our ghost is just not a cat lover."

"Wanda, this is getting too weird." I shook my head. "Stop saying these things."

"OK, kid." Wanda turned to go. "Anyway, I wouldn't share this conversation with your mom. She'd probably decide to move, and I've finally got everything in the studio set up the way I want it. I can put up with a singing ghost."

She was right about Mom. Mom was already uptight about meeting up with a cockroach from one of the cupboards. But like Wanda, it would kill her to move. We'd never find another place close to the university, and it would cost too much money if we did.

"There's no ghost!" I shouted down the echoing hall after Wanda. She didn't call back. All I could hear was the sound of her thumping up the stairs and her studio door banging shut.

But that night, I couldn't sleep. I was aware of every creak and groan in the house. There was also the noise of nearby Bloor Street. Horns honking and tires squealing, and sometimes shouting and laughing from the all-night restaurant on the corner. I kept checking the red numbers on my clock. Finally I must have dozed off, because the numbers read 3:32 when I woke up with a jolt, my heart pounding.

Something was thumping down the attic stairs one step at a time, just the way Wanda had described the ghost. Shuffling footsteps approached my door. I clenched my teeth so hard, I thought my jaw would snap. Then the shuffling stopped. There was a sudden cry. Something hard and round rolled down the hallway, faster and faster, heading toward the kitchen. Then silence. I lay there shivering, too scared to get up and look, but too scared to sleep either.

In the morning I checked all around the kitchen, looking for a hard, round object. There was nothing there. But I was sure I'd heard something. I raced up the attic stairs and pounded on Wanda's door. When she grunted, I shoved it open. The slanted walls were covered with art. The floor was covered in clothes and painting supplies. Wanda grinned sleepily at me from her futon on the floor. "Well, Karen, did you hear it? Was I right?"

I nodded. "You were right," I mumbled. I noticed she wore her crystal necklace even in bed.

"You bet. It's a ghost, like I said." She snuggled back down in her heap of quilts and cushions. "Now, let me sleep."

Maybe Wanda could sleep, but I couldn't. I lay awake

every night, watching the car lights travel across the cracked ceiling, listening for the shuffling footsteps and the sound of something small and hard rolling past my door. It was usually after three when the noises started. While I waited, I picked at the layers of old wallpaper beside my bed. I peeled back horrible red velvet paper, then pink roses, then blue stripes. I was down to wallpaper with green ferns when I got sick.

It was the middle of my mom's mid-term exams. I knew how important they were to her, so I got Wanda to take me to the doctor. We took the subway, even though it wasn't very far. The doctor scribbled out a prescription and handed it to Wanda. "Take this up to the drugstore at the corner of Davenport and Dupont. Their prices are better." I guess he could see we weren't rich.

That meant a bus ride, and slogging through blocks of slushy snow, but we went. It was an old-fashioned drugstore, with medicine bottles in the window. The druggist read the prescription. "Eighty-three Clinton Street!" He looked delighted, as if we were old friends. "My best friend, Billy Reid, used to live in that house," he said, leaning his elbows on the counter.

My legs felt ready to collapse, and I was cold. All I wanted to do was get home and back to bed, but the druggist kept talking. "Billy's grandfather used to live upstairs in the attic. You know, when he died, it was a terrible loss for Billy. Such a shock! The family moved soon after. . . ."

"Why?" Wanda asked, cocking her head to one side. "How did he die?"

The druggist shook some pills into a plastic container. "Why, he fell down all those stairs from the attic," he said. "I remember how narrow and steep they were, too! Grandpa Reid . . ." The druggist paused, remembering. "We used to have so much fun in that house. Billy and I would set up a game of marbles in that long hall on the second floor — you know the one?" We nodded in unison. ". . . and old Grandpa Reid could shoot a steely with the best of us. Those steel balls would go whizzing down the hall and smack into the door of Billy's mother's sewing room. She would come storming out, yelling with her mouth full of pins!" He shook his head, laughing.

I felt as though my brain would explode. Marbles. That's what I was hearing at night. Marbles rolling down the hall. Kids my age, playing marbles with an old man. A man who died falling down the stairs!

"How long ago was this?" Wanda demanded. I could feel her excitement.

"Well," the druggist answered, "I'm nearly ready to retire, so that would be more than fifty years ago. But I remember that old man as if it were yesterday."

"Did he like to sing?" Wanda asked. She was almost jumping up and down.

"Oh, sure! He was full of funny old songs and sayings

from Ireland. Some of them weren't too polite, mind you. He'd teach them to us when Billy's mother wasn't listening." The druggist smiled. "I remember one . . ." He started singing,

> *Not last night, but the night before,*
> *Three young tomcats came to the door.*
> *One had a fiddle, and one had a drum,*
> *And one had a pancake stuck to his . . .*

He stopped, suddenly embarrassed. "I'd forgotten all about Grandpa Reid's singing." The druggist pushed his glasses back up his nose. "Well, here's your prescription. Did you say you were on a drug plan?"

"No. No drug plan," Wanda told him. I could tell she was in a hurry to leave.

"I'll give you a good deal, just for old time's sake. Say hello to the old house on Clinton for me."

"We will," Wanda said. When we were finally outside, she grabbed my coat sleeve. "That's our ghost!" she shouted. "Grandpa Reid!"

"Grandpa Reid." I tried to imagine him as we plodded down the snowy street, but my brain was numb. It had got dark while we were in the drugstore. The cold was cutting right through my thin coat like icy scissors.

I felt so strange and dizzy by the time we got back to 83 Clinton that I could hardly get up the porch steps.

Nothing seemed real. Maybe I had dreamed the whole thing in the drugstore, I thought. Just to be sure, before I let Wanda tuck me into bed, I checked the kitchen doorframe for hinges. There they were, under layers of old paint. The kitchen could have been a sewing room!

I moved over to the kitchen window. I was always hoping for a sign of Toby. Maybe she was out there, freezing and miserable, afraid to come in. Maybe if I called her just one more time.

I opened the back door and stumbled out on the tiny porch in my pajamas and stocking feet. "TOBY!" I called into the frosty air. "Here, Toby. Here, cat!"

From a high, bare maple I heard, "Meow."

"TOBY!" I took a step forward, slipped on the ice, and grabbed for the railing. Normally I'm very coordinated, but my head was whirling with fever. The railing seemed to give way under my arm. I felt myself hurtling down that long, ice-coated flight of stairs. A voice came floating down behind me.

> The higher up the mountain,
> the greener grows the grass.
> Down came a billy-goat,
> sliding on his . . . overcoat.

The voice enveloped me. I felt wiry arms clutching at me, catching me, holding me up. "Dang stairs." It was a gravelly, old voice. "They'll be the death of me someday. . . ."

Then the voice faded away. I was alone, sitting on an icy, frozen step about halfway down, sobbing for breath and clutching the railing for all I was worth. But I was warm, warm all over, as though I'd just stepped out of a hot bath.

"Karen!" Wanda shrieked. "Oh my god, are you all right?" She came thundering down the stairs behind me.

"Watch the railing," I said. "It's not too solid." I was as calm as if I were sitting on the stairs on a warm summer's day.

"What were you doing out here?" Wanda was almost hysterical.

I had to think for a minute before I could remember. "I was after Toby. I heard her. Wanda, look!" I pointed up at the porch railing.

Toby was waiting for us there, her tail curled neatly around her body. When I made a grab for her, she leaped lightly down and rubbed against my leg, asking to go inside.

Later, when I was wrapped up in bed with sweet tea on my table and a warm cat on my stomach, Wanda came in with her sketch pad. She sat cross-legged on the floor. "Just hold that pose," she said.

I still have her portrait of me and Toby curled up together. Late that same night I heard rustling noises outside my room. This time I got up to see what they were. I opened my door slowly and peered down the dark hall. A shape came dashing out of the shadows and pounced. I gasped. It was only Toby, chasing dustballs in the dark.

Wanda and I never again heard singing or footsteps on the stairs. In June Mom finally got her degree and we all moved away from Clinton Street. Last summer, when we were back in the neighborhood for Wanda's graduation, we walked past the old house. Number 83 is a Chinese acupuncture center now. It looks different. It seems funny to think we don't live there any more, and can't just open the door and walk in. I thought I saw a face in the attic window, but it may have just been one of the patients. I wonder if Grandpa Reid is watching out for them on the stairs?

• • •

Brian Doyle

CARROT CAKE

My friend Kenny loves it when the clocks have to be changed. There's lots of fun to be had in getting people to talk about the clocks changing and what happens when they do change. Fun to be had in getting people to try and remember if it's "Fall Back, Spring Ahead" or the other way around, "Fall Ahead, Spring Back." Or in getting people mixed up by saying things like: "I guess we saved an hour last night when we put the clocks ahead," and making other people start to argue about it — "No, you don't save an hour, you lose an hour," or "Yes, you do, that's just another hour you don't have to put up with," or "If you wake up in the morning and the clock says eight o'clock but it's really nine o'clock and you're late for work, does that mean you've lost an hour or you've gained an hour?" and "Sometimes my mother puts the clock back before she goes to sleep and my father gets up in the morning and puts it back, too, and then *nobody* knows what time it is!"

And sometimes Kenny will get people thinking about their VCRs. Kenny will say things like "If you've got a late-late movie being taped on your VCR, and at three o'clock in the morning it's all of a sudden two o'clock in the morning, does that mean that part of the movie gets taped all over again?"

Kenny says that even their dog, Nerves the Ninth, gets very confused when the clocks get changed.

Nerves the Ninth is descended from Nerves the First, a famous Canadian dog who helped save a covered bridge up around the town of Low, Quebec, near Ottawa, from being torn down way back in 1950. Nerves the First was a funny-looking little dog who had a personality something like a mirror. He always tried to get in the same mood as the people around him.

Nerves the Ninth has a very similar personality. On the morning the clocks get turned ahead, Nerves the Ninth goes around most of the day half-asleep. And on the day the clocks get put back, Nerves the Ninth is so wide awake in the morning that his little beady eyes with the long eyelashes are open twice as wide as usual.

Kenny pretends to have a theory that when the clocks are put back on the last Sunday in October, everybody gets an hour younger, everybody goes back in time. And that means that you go back to where you were an hour ago and that what happened in the last hour of your life never really happened at all.

Kenny also pretends that what you see is actually not really there. Our science teacher, Hem, got her started on that. He told us one day that molecules are constantly changing, and since people are made up of molecules, people are never the same from one minute to the next. Hem also told us that a lot of the stars we see in the sky aren't even there, because it takes the light so long to get to Earth that the stars have moved already or exploded or disappeared years ago. Then he made the mistake of telling us that since light takes some time to travel from an object to your eye, that object isn't exactly right where you think you see it.

"Does that mean," Kenny asked Hem, "that my friend Dorothy over there, who I'm looking at, isn't really exactly there?" Kenny means me, Dorothy Del Rose.

"Pretty much," said the science teacher. Then he said, "HEM!"

I have to tell you about our science teacher, Hem. Most people, when they clear their throats, make a double, polite sound that goes "ahem." Some people, often teachers, do "ahem" quietly, to get your attention. Or if they are mad, they might go "AHEM!"

Our science teacher has a habit of clearing his throat like this: "HEM!" We don't think he realizes he's doing it. We think that it's just some kind of nervous habit, that he doesn't even need his throat cleared. He does it like a grunt or the short bark of a big dog. It's a deep sound and quite loud. He might even do a few for you as he comes down the hall and turns into the room. He does it so often that everybody calls him Hem. He does it so much, in fact, that most people don't even notice any more. But one day Kenny reminded everybody about it.

Kenny got twenty-five pieces of paper and wrote numbers on them. It was a pool. You paid a quarter and chose a number. If you picked the right number of "HEMs!" Hem did in one period of science, you'd win. The winner would get five dollars.

The twenty-five pieces of paper were sold in five minutes. What a great idea! Kenny would make $1.25 profit.

I drew the ticket that said, "Any number over twenty-five." The best ticket. It was just luck. That day Hem went "HEM!" thirty-eight times — thirty-nine if you counted the one he gave us in the hall just before he came in. I won the five dollars and Kenny made $1.25 profit.

Everybody was mad. They said it was fixed, 'specially some of the boys. They were saying girls shouldn't be running gambling things anyway. See, my friend Kenny's real name is Kendra-Anne. Kendra-Anne Kavanaugh.

Anyway, all this stuff about things that you see aren't really there, and about how nothing is exactly what it was like a few seconds ago, gave Kenny an idea. She decided we'd go over to my place on the night they turn the clocks back and have a little fun.

Here's what happened.

It's the last Saturday of October, the night they put the clocks back, and Kenny is staying over at my house because her father, who is an undercover agent, is having a secret meeting at her place.

I live on Rowanwood Avenue, the street with all the rowanwood trees. The trees have little clumps of berries that hang there so red in the winter time, with a little white roof of snow on each clump in January, until all of a sudden about a thousand birds show up and knock the snow off and make a huge fuss while they eat every single berry off every single rowanwood tree on Rowanwood Avenue, and then they take off somewhere until next year.

But this isn't January, this is the end of October, and Kenny and I are awake and waiting for it to be three o'clock in the morning so we can turn the clocks back.

Kenny has a plan.

All this talk about stars not really being there, friends changing before your eyes because of molecules, hours disappearing, dogs going around half-asleep because they don't know what time it is, has made Kenny a little strange tonight. Tonight, says Kenny, we're going to create the carrot cake that never was! Kenny and I make the best carrot cake in Ottawa West. We're a team. First,

I get out some carrots and an apple. I wash the carrots and grate them up until we have a cupful. I don't peel them. Then I grate up the apple. While I'm doing this, Kenny's got out the big bowl and in goes a cup of vegetable oil. Then four eggs. Then a cup of sugar. She beats it up by hand until it's yellow. I get a smaller aluminum bowl and put in a cup of white flour, a cup of whole wheat flour, a teaspoon of cinnamon, some salt, some baking powder, some baking soda. Then Kenny gets out the big, Pyrex lasagna pan and butters it up with butter.

Next, I pour the stuff from the aluminum bowl into the big bowl. Kenny mixes and puts in the carrots and the apple. Then I mix. Then I turn on the oven to 175°C. Kenny puts it all into the lasagna dish and I spread it out. Then Kenny puts it in the oven and I set the timer for thirty-five minutes. What a team! Fifteen minutes is all it takes to make the cake!

But Kenny says we can't start until two o'clock, so we've got some time to kill.

There's not much on TV, so I get out my favorite video tapes. My Dad bought me them for Christmas. Kenny likes these tapes too. We make some popcorn and settle into the big, comfortable couch. The first movie, *Psycho*, is in black and white. With our remote, we settle back with the popcorn and fast-forward and rewind and repeat all the good parts.

Of course we fast-forward to the famous shower

scene, where Norman Bates does the job on Marian Crane. Then we find the part where Norman is arguing with his dead mother and we try our imitations of the shower-scene music. It's not really music, it's sort of a high, *squeet-squeet-squeet!* sound. Next, we fast-forward to where the detective is coming up the stairs and then you hear the *squeet-squeet!* and Norman's mother comes tearing out and knifes him. We find the part where the sheriff reveals that Norman Bates's mother has been DEAD for years! And then we skip to the end where Norman is locked up in the nut house and the fly is crawling across his hand. While the fly is crawling, Kenny and I go *squeet-squeet-squeet!* but not too loud. We don't want to wake my parents up.

I get up and put on *Psycho II*, the one we like the best. At the end Norman asks the woman visiting in his kitchen, Mrs. Spool, "You're sure you won't have a sandwich?" and then goes behind her and whacks her across the head with a shovel, using the shovel like a baseball bat. We fast-forward through the first part, where they let Norman Bates out of the nut house, and we start watching it where that slimy Warren Toomey gets stabbed by somebody dressed as Norman's mom. The knife going in again and again sounds like stabbing soft ice. "Mother! Oh God! Mother! Blood!" We decide to let the film run without skipping. Horror is better if you lead up to it slowly.

A bit later Kenny checks her watch. It's five to two, time to start creating the carrot cake that never was. In an hour the cake will be done, we'll turn back the clock, and presto! It never happened!

We get right down to it.

I start washing and grating the carrots and Kenny gets out the big bowl and puts in the vegetable oil and the eggs. Then the doorbell rings. Who could that be at ten after two in the morning? I wipe the red, grated carrot juice off my fingers and go into the dark living room, where *Psycho III* is now quietly showing. I look out the living-room window to see who's standing at the door. I can't make anybody out. I go to the front door and peek out. I turn on the veranda light. Nobody. On the TV screen the sheriff, who likes Norman, is taking an ice cube out of the freezer at the Bates Motel. The ice cube the sheriff puts in his mouth has blood on it. Not surprising. The freezer contains one of Norman's corpses.

When I get back in the kitchen, Kenny's got the wooden spoon in the bowl, but she's not beating the eggs and the oil and the sugar. And she's got a strange look on her face. There's someone sitting at the kitchen table.

"HEM!" he says.

I go straight up off the floor.

By the time I get back down, the skin of my whole body feels like a plucked goose. "Mr. Hogan is here," Kenny says, giving me a look I've never seen before.

"It's all right," says Hem Hogan, our science teacher. "Your mother and father will be here in a few minutes. We were all at the Hunt Club's final executive meeting and your folks invited a few of us over for a nightcap." Hem looks a little glassy-eyed, like most of our parents do when they get home from those golf club "executive meetings." And there is something drastically wrong with what he has just said. My parents aren't at any golf club. They are up in bed.

Kenny is looking at me over the big bowl with the wooden spoon in her hand. There is a message of terror in her eyes.

"Just a minute, Mr. Hogan," I say. "I'll go and get my father."

As I leave the kitchen, I can hear Kenny furiously beating the sides of the bowl. And Hem going "HEM!"

He must be drunk, I'm thinking to myself as I climb the stairs. We live in a big house and our stairs are long. On TV Norman is killing Dwayne Duke by beating him over the head with his own guitar. The hall light upstairs is usually on until everybody's in bed. But tonight, for some reason, it's off. Hem Hogan probably has this night mixed up with some other one. I know my parents are upstairs in bed. In fact, they wanted us to save them some of the carrot cake that never was, that we were going to cook in the hour that never was, between two and three in the morning when we put the clocks back.

My parents' bedroom is the big one at the front of the house. There's a beautiful view from the balcony, of the Ottawa River and the Gatineau Hills and the rowan-wood trees.

I open my parents' bedroom door and a rush of cool air blows through me. The balcony door is wide open and the October moonlight is pouring in over the empty bed. A deafening swarm of vicious birds is ripping the rowan-wood trees to tattered shreds. Hem is right. My parents aren't there.

It doesn't seem possible.

As I rush down the stairs, Norman Bates, on the TV screen, is screaming "MOTHER!" because his dead mother, who he has stuffed like one of his birds, has caused him to murder one too many innocent bystanders with his butcher knife.

From the kitchen the sound of mixing is louder and faster now. I rush in, but I'm stopped cold.

Hem is now mixing the carrot cake. His eyes look wild. There's cake batter flying all over the place. And another thing.

Hem is wearing a woman's wig and a dress!

And another thing.

Kenny's gone!

"HEM! SIT DOWN!" says Hem. "Dorothy Del Rose," he continues, while he pours the carrot cake batter into the glass pan, "you and your friend, HEM!

Kendra-Anne, HEM! have been making a lot of fun of me, haven't you? HEM! I don't think that's, HEM! funny."

Beside the pan of batter is our long butcher knife with the carrot juice on it, or is it something else? Hem uses the knife to smooth out the batter in the pan. He licks it off. Then he picks up the pan and sticks the knife in front of my face. "HEM! Let's go in and show this cake to your little friend Kendra-Anne Kavanaugh before we put it in the oven, HEM! OK?"

We go into the living room and come up behind the couch. Kenny's sleeping on her side, facing the TV. "HEM! Kendra-Anne!" shouts Hem. "Here's your favorite friend with your favorite CAKE!" He reaches over the back of the couch and yanks Kenny by the shoulder.

She rolls over onto her back.

Her throat is bubbling blood from a wide, jagged gash.

Hem pours the carrot-cake batter into the gurgling wound of her throat. "Motherrrrrr!" I'm screaming.

I wake up sitting up on the couch. Kenny is sitting up too. The TV is humming, the screen snowy. I switch off the VCR, take out the tape of *Psycho II* (we never did get to see *Psycho III*), and switch to the time channel. The time on the TV is one minute past two. Our watches say one minute past three. We don't even bother to put our watches back. We've missed the hour anyway. Everything is ruined. No cake. No nothing. We go up to bed. It never happened.

I'm sitting on the edge of the bed pulling off my socks and listening to Kenny complaining about missing the hour and saying now we'll have to wait until April before we get to move the clocks again and will it be back, or forward, she forgets.

I think I hear some noise coming from my parents' bedroom. Now there's shouting and I hear my mother screaming, and then the whole house is shaking and now crashing through the clothes-closet door is Hem and he soars across the room and plunges his bread knife into my heart while Kenny laughs and shouts, "HEM! HEM!" as her face turns green and her teeth fall clattering to the floor and her arms and legs fall off!

Then I *do* wake up downstairs on the couch, the TV humming and snowy. I'm howling and Kenny is shaking me. What a night!

Now, in science class, even though I know it's coming, every time I hear "HEM!" I jump, my heart stops, I catch my breath, and my flesh goes all goosey.

• • •

Monica Hughes

THE HAUNTING
OF THE ORION QUEEN

The star cruiser *Orion Queen* had always been a clean, well-run ship, and Captain Mirador was proud of every meter of it, from the sleek consoles in the control room to the neat plastiwood paneling of the crew's quarters along the starboard gangway and the passenger quarters on the port side. He reveled in the quiet hum of the thrusters as they sweetly drove his ship through the galaxy, and in the sight of the huge cargo bay, its pods neatly packed from floor to ceiling with farm machinery, seeds, cryogenically frozen sheep, and all the other necessities for the new colony on the planet Obduran.

Captain Mirador would have been a lot happier if the fifteen orphan children he had been ordered to take along could have been put into cryogenic suspension as well and stacked in a cargo pod with the sheep. "I hate kids," he protested to the port authorities on Earth. "They don't belong on a star ship."

But the authorities insisted. The children were nothing but unwanted mouths to feed down on Earth. On a young colony they would be extra muscle power. Though they were not paying passengers, they were to be treated as such.

"Just keep them out of my way, Number One," the captain snapped at First Officer Haprin.

Judy Haprin did her best, but it wasn't easy, given the children's age ranges. Anthea and Bill, who were fourteen, were the oldest, but Natalie and Madeline were only eight. They had comic books to read, as well as a stock of books for the new colony's library, and the first officer taught them card games in her spare time. But with three to a cabin and a passengers' lounge no more than five by four meters, something had to give.

"You can play along the port gangway," the first officer told them. "But stay away from the starboard side and out of the captain's hair. All right?"

The *Orion Queen* was three Earth-calendar months away from Obduran when the trouble started. Judy Haprin was walking along the starboard gangway when she encountered a man dressed in a blue jacket, tight breeches, and a three-cornered hat.

"Hey, where do you think you're going?" demanded the first officer. "And who in space are you?"

"Pieces of eight, pieces of eight."

The first officer blinked. Had the large green bird on

the man's shoulder said that? "Now you see here . . ."

The man ignored her. She could hear him singing as he went: "Fifteen men on a dead man's chest. Yo, ho, ho and a bottle of rum."

"Wait!" she shouted. But though he had a wooden stump in place of one leg, he was gone by the time she reached the turn in the passage. "I must be going space crazy," she muttered and reported to sick bay.

"So what's the trouble, Judy?" Doctor Biggs asked.

The first officer opened her mouth to describe the one-legged man and the talking bird, but when she saw the doctor's hand poised over her chart, she shut her mouth again. She could imagine what the diagnosis would look like in her annual report.

"Well?" the doctor asked once more.

"Nothing, really. Just a bit edgy."

"Hmm. That's not like you. I can give you a shot of neurorelaxant if you like." Doctor Biggs filled a syringe and held it against the first officer's neck. "Don't know what's wrong with the crew the last couple of days. I'm almost out of this stuff. If it goes on like this, we'll be back to . . ." She was interrupted by a series of piercing yells. "What the . . . ?"

By the time the first officer and the doctor had followed the sound across the ship to the port gangway, a large crowd had collected. Natalie Pushkin was lying in the middle of it, drumming her heels on the metal floor and screaming. Doctor Biggs pushed through the crowd, picked her up, and took her to sick bay. She gave Natalie a shot of neurorelaxant, one of the last in her supply, listened to her ravings, and went to see Captain Mirador.

"I knew there'd be trouble with a cargo of kids!" he ranted.

"Only fifteen of them, sir."

"Fifteen or fifty, they're still trouble. Is the child able to talk coherently?"

"I suppose. . . ."

"Then send all fifteen to my office, Doctor. And call Number One."

"What's up?" whispered Anthea to her friend Bill as the children filed down the corridor and into the captain's office. "He looks awfully mad."

"Silence," snarled Captain Mirador. "Be seated. You . . . Natalie Pushkin. Inform the court of inquiry of what you saw."

Natalie sniffed and hiccupped. "It was a horrible man, sir. In funny clothes."

"Did he have a green parrot on his shoulder?" the first officer found herself asking. Sixteen pairs of eyes turned to her, and she blushed and dropped her pen.

"Does that question have any particular significance, Number One?" asked the captain sarcastically.

"N-no, sir. Sorry, sir." Her voice shook and she took a deep breath.

"Carry on, Natalie. What did the man do?"

"Nothing, sir. He . . . he just smiled." She shuddered violently.

"Is that *all*? You made that appalling row for *that*?"

"But, sir . . . His head, sir . . ."

"Smiled."

"Yes, sir. But it wasn't on his shoulders, sir. It was under his *arm*." Natalie burst into tears.

Captain Mirador glared at the other fourteen children. "I might have known it. Trouble! Which of you dressed up to frighten Natalie? Speak up at once or you will be severely punished."

The children stared blankly at each other. "Maybe he'll make us walk the plank," Bill whispered and Anthea snorted.

"Who said that? You, boy, speak up."

"I just said you might make us walk the plank, sir. It was a joke, sir. Like pirates in the old stories."

Pirates. The word jolted the first officer's memory of her apparition. A wooden leg. And a talking parrot. The kids couldn't have done *that*, could they? And if not them, then who? Or *what*? She looked down and found she had written on her note pad: "Yo, ho, ho and a bottle of rum." She crossed it out hastily. I am *not* going crazy, she told herself firmly.

The captain glared at Bill. "You look like the oldest. What have you to say about it? A game, is that what it was? Speak up now."

"It's nothing to do with us, sir. Honest. We don't have anything to dress up in, even if we did want to scare Natalie."

"That's true enough," put in the first officer. "The young people have only what they are wearing plus one change of clothing for onboard use. Everything else is stowed away in cargo."

"They *must* be guilty. Own up. Who frightened Natalie?"

The children looked blankly at each other and at the captain.

"Very well. Minimum rations until I get a confession."

"But, sir, you can't do that," protested First Officer Haprin.

"Can't I, indeed? They're not registered as paying passengers, they're registered as cargo. If I had my way, that's where they'd be. Minimum rations."

I should tell him about the one-legged pirate, thought First Officer Haprin. *"Space crazy," that's what he'll say.* "Go back to your quarters, children," she said flatly.

Meekly they filed out behind the officers' chairs.

". . . and if you hadn't made such a stupid fuss, Talie," Bill said as soon as they were back in their own living area, squabbling for seats on the settees that lined the walls or sitting cross-legged on the tiled floor, "we wouldn't be in this mess. Nutribars and water twice a day. Yuck!"

"I couldn't help it. Honest. If you'd seen it, you'd have yelled too. It was gross!"

"It's a mystery, that's what it is. And it's up to us to investigate it," said Anthea practically. "Look for clues and stuff like that. Talie, tell us again."

"Well, he was wearing a funny red jacket with tears in the sleeves and his shirt poking out of them. And he had a collar that stood out all round as big as a plate and . . . and . . ." She gulped.

"Don't start again, Talie, or you'll get this pitcher of water over your head," Anthea warned.

"You wouldn't."

"Try me. Come on, you'd got to his collar."

"His neck was sticking out of it, and there was a trickle of blood down the front of his throat."

Madeline LeBlanc screeched. "Was his head really . . . ? How gross!"

Natalie nodded. "Under his arm, with its eyes shut. Then . . . then the eyes opened and stared, like they were really seeing me. And he smiled. I could s-see his t-teeth shining. So I screamed."

"I take it back," said Bill. "I'd have screamed too."

"It's a headless ghost," Mark Harrison said in a dramatic voice and the smaller ones screeched again. Natalie began to cry.

"A ghost? On a star cruiser? That's crazy," Bill objected.

"Maybe it was a hologram," suggested Ollie Olafsen.

"That makes more sense. Only who set it up? And why did they do it? Just to scare Talie?"

"Maybe it's a psychological test, something they do to you when you go to a space colony."

"Who'd want to give us tests, Ollie? We're just going to grow up to be farmers."

Anthea sighed. "This isn't getting us anywhere. We're going to have to find out exactly what's going on and fast! We don't want to stay on minimum rations any longer, do we?"

"Listen, kids," said Bill. "You've got to stay together in twos and threes from now on, just in case the headless man appears again and we have to prove that it wasn't us. So no wandering off on your own. Anthea and I'll look for clues."

"If I see him again, I'll just die," moaned Natalie.

"No, you won't. You'll know it's just a hologram. Stick your tongue out at it. That'll show whoever's playing this game on us that we're not taken in," Anthea said encouragingly.

"I can't wait." Bill rubbed his hands together.

Two days later Captain Mirador was strolling from his private quarters to the bridge, mellow after eight hours of uninterrupted sleep. He felt he had handled the rebellious children rather well. Suddenly he became aware of an unfamiliar figure ahead of him. "Halt! Who goes there? You're in restricted quarters."

The person sauntered on as if he had not heard.

At first glance the captain had thought he was in white coveralls, but now he could see that the stranger was swathed in bandages from head to foot. An accident? Burn victim? But surely Doctor Biggs would have notified him. "Identify yourself. That's an order." He stood in front of the figure, barring its way. The dark glasses that hid the eyes gave the bandaged face an insolent look. Captain Mirador reached up and snatched them off. "I said identify yourself, mister. I . . ."

His throat tightened and his mouth was suddenly dry, for behind the glasses there were no eyes, not even the horror of empty sockets. He was looking at . . . nothing. Where skin and bone and brain should have been, he could see the concave shape of the wrappings at the back of the person's head. From the *inside*.

Captain Mirador yelled and ran. Doors opened and crew members stared. Wordlessly he pointed behind him, saw the bewilderment on their faces, and turned. The white figure had vanished.

He pulled himself together. "Search the ship," he snapped.

"Sir! . . . What for, sir?"

"Intruders. Kids dressed up. Oh, use your intelligence. Just search!" He stamped onto the bridge. "They've been at it again," he snarled at the duty officer. "Those brats, trying to scare people with Halloween masks. That's it!

Just papier-mâché masks. But I got the glasses. I'll nail those kids with fingerprints this time."

He placed the dark glasses on the console in front of him. As soon as they were out of his hand they began to fade, glass and frame alike, to a pale gray, then a paler gray. In a moment they no longer cast a shadow on the white console top. They were like a wisp of smoke. Then they vanished.

Captain Mirador pointed a shaking finger. "D'you see that?"

"I . . . I don't see anything, sir," stammered the duty officer.

"Moron! Did you see what it was before it wasn't there?"

"A . . . a pair of sunglasses, sir?"

Captain Mirador snorted. "Some sort of conjuring trick. Get me those children!"

"*Now*, sir? It's only six in the morning."

"*Now*. This minute. In my office. And call Number One."

At the door of his office Captain Mirador was confronted not by the children, but by First Officer Judy Haprin. "The duty officer reported that you'd ordered the children to be woken for a court of inquiry. That is ridiculous, sir. They have all been in their beds since ten last night."

"Not all of them, I'll bet. Running around wrapped in sheets with papier-mâché masks!"

"You're wrong, sir. And I'll swear to it in court."

The captain groaned. Even his first officer had turned against him. It was more than he could cope with before his first cup of coffee.

By breakfast time every person on the *Orion Queen* knew that the mysterious stranger had struck again. The crew looked distrustfully at each other and went about their work silently, stopping occasionally to look over their shoulders suspiciously.

"It can't be one person, Bill," argued Anthea. "First a man with his head under his arm. Now a person with no head at all." *And what about the parrot?* she asked herself, suddenly remembering the odd behavior of the first officer during the court of inquiry. She went to investigate and found Haprin in the saloon, brooding over a cup of coffee. She sat down beside her.

"Yo, ho, ho and a bottle of rum," Anthea said softly.

First Officer Haprin jumped violently and spilled hot coffee all over her hand. "So it *was* you kids after all. How did you do the one-legged pirate? Where did you get that bird? And how did you get out of your cabins last night? I locked you in."

"It wasn't us. Honest."

"Then how d'you know about . . . 'yo, ho, ho' and all that?" The first officer lowered her voice.

"I saw it on your note pad when we left the captain's office. And after Bill talked about pirates, you said something about a parrot. You've seen something too, haven't you? Why didn't you tell the captain at the court of inquiry? He'd know we couldn't have got hold of a parrot, and then maybe he wouldn't have put us on half rations."

"And have him call me space crazy? I want to captain a star cruiser myself one day. That'll never happen with a bad medical report."

"You're no more space crazy than the captain, are you? He saw a man with no head. I wish you'd tell me exactly what you did see. It could be useful. Bill and I are collecting clues."

First Officer Haprin looked at her doubtfully. "I suppose I might as well. . . ."

After she'd heard the story, Anthea sighed. "It makes no sense at all. Are you sure it's not being done with holograms?"

"Of course not. We have no equipment like that on board. Why would we?"

"To test us kids, we thought. But if it's not that, it's got to be ghosts, and you'll *have* to tell the captain."

Once the first officer had confessed to what she had seen, the captain grimly interrogated the entire crew and, at last, the extent of the haunting was finally revealed. One by one, on pain of instant dismissal, at least a third of the crew admitted glimpsing green slime or blood dripping from the bulkheads, white wailing figures flitting along the gangways, and other bizarre apparitions. There was no doubt about it. The *Orion Queen* was lousy with ghosts. And the crew was dangerously jittery.

An urgent message to Earth brought the following cryptic response: *Try exorcism.*

"Nonsense," stuttered Captain Mirador. "I've never heard of anything so outrageous. I don't believe . . . I won't believe . . ."

"But, sir, the ghosts are here. And the crew's morale is getting worse by the day. It'll be ten weeks before we make landfall in Obduran. By then . . ." First Officer Haprin shook her head. "We can't risk someone having a real mental breakdown. The doctor's already got more cases of nerves in sick bay than she can handle. If one of the crew should go berserk, we could have a nasty accident on our hands. We've got to do something."

Captain Mirador sighed heavily and called the ship's chaplain. "Try exorcism," he ordered briefly.

"I . . . I beg your pardon, sir?"

"You know what exorcism is, don't you? It's a religious rite to get rid of ghosts." The captain swallowed. "We have ghosts. Get rid of them."

"I've never . . . I don't really know the form . . ." The chaplain's voice faded at the look in Captain Mirador's eyes, and he left the bridge hastily.

Half an hour later, walking the main gangway with a lit candle in one hand and a bell in the other, the chaplain slipped in a newly manifested blob of green slime and cracked his shin. The candle went out. He got to his feet and limped on, ringing the bell until, just outside sick bay, he encountered a hideous hunchback clothed in nineteenth-century rags. He shut his eyes and swallowed. "Begone, unquiet spirit," he stammered. When he opened his eyes, the hunchback was smiling at him. The chaplain moaned and checked himself into sick bay.

"What do we do now?" Captain Mirador asked the first officer. "The shipping line has no other bright ideas. Exorcism indeed! I knew it wouldn't work. It's those children. I've never carried children before. It *must* have something to do with them. But how? And why?"

In the passengers' lounge Bill and Anthea had come to the same conclusion. "Do you think we brought something aboard with us? A stray poltergeist, maybe?" Anthea suggested.

"They only throw stuff around, don't they? And they've no imagination," objected Bill. "D'you know, I saw something that looked like Darth Vadar at the end of the corridor near engineering."

"Who?"

"Don't be ignorant, Anthea. A villain out of an old, old comic book called *Star Wars*."

Anthea stared and then slapped the table with the flat

of her hand. "Comics, of course! I couldn't figure out where the green slime was coming from. You've got it, Bill. We're being haunted by our books." She began rummaging through the antique books the children were taking to the colony library. "A one-legged pirate . . . an invisible man . . . and a headless ghost." She tossed three books onto the table. "*The Invisible Man* by H. G. Wells. See the picture on the cover? And the pirate in *Treasure Island*." She picked up one of the books and leafed through the pages. "Just listen to this:

> *There, advancing from the door of the powdering-room, a figure in doublet and hose, a ruff round its neck — and no head! The head, sure enough, was there; but it was under the right arm, held close in the slashed-velvet sleeve of the doublet. The face looking from under the arm wore a pleasant smile.*

"That's it," screamed Natalie. "That's what I saw."

"But it's just a novel," Ollie put in. "*The Enchanted Castle*. I was reading it last week. Not bad."

"I don't understand," said Bill. "Do you mean whoever is testing us is getting the ideas out of our books?"

"I don't know. First Officer Haprin says they weren't — testing us, I mean. And she should know. But if it isn't holograms, then it really is ghosts, isn't it?" She shivered. "Somehow they're coming out of our books. We've got to tell the captain what we've found out."

"Do we dare? He still thinks it's our fault."

"You don't want to stay on water and nutribars another day, do you? After all, what else can he do to us? Come on, fellow detective, let's confront him with the evidence."

Anthea dumped the books by the captain's chair on the bridge. "You see, here's the man in bandages. And this is Natalie's ghost."

The first officer picked up *Treasure Island* and stared at the picture on the cover. "This is exactly like the one-legged pirate with the parrot that I saw!"

"It's a ridiculous idea," snapped Captain Mirador. "How can my ship be haunted by imaginary characters out of a collection of old books?"

"Hold on, sir," the first officer interrupted. "I think maybe Anthea here is onto something. A wandering space entity. We know they exist, Captain. I'll bet you've been aboard a ship where one of them glitched the computer. Luckily they only survive out in space. As soon as a ship approaches a planet, they leave."

"I've never *seen* one, though. Seeing is believing, First Officer."

"Space entities have no corporeal bodies. You *can't* see them. But suppose these children brought some different kind of energy aboard with them, something powerful enough to permit this entity to adopt the physical appearance of the characters in their books?"

The captain looked thoughtful. "No, that won't work. It's never happened before and there are plenty of books around." He waved his hand at the *Star Atlas*, *The History of Space Colonization*, and *Who's Who in the Galaxy*, all gathering dust on a shelf. "Used to look at them myself once."

"Maybe our books are more interesting," suggested Bill.

"Imagination," said the first officer. "That's it, sir!"

"Imagination?" Captain Mirador stared blankly. "What has imagination to do with anything?"

"Everything, I think. I'm sure Anthea is right. Her theory fits the facts: the kind of hauntings, each appearance traceable to a book that some, if not all, of the youngsters have read. They invest their reading with imagination, and the space entity has sucked up that energy to give itself a physical appearance."

"Never heard of such a thing," grumbled Captain Mirador.

"We are carrying young people for the first time."

"And the last. So what do you suggest we do?"

"We could starve the entity by destroying all the books . . ."

"Oh, no," Anthea cried. "You can't!"

"Great idea, Number One. Incinerate the books. That should do it."

"But you can't destroy our books, sir. They're for the colony," protested Anthea.

"And we're bound to go on thinking about what we've read. You can't just turn off our imaginations like a tap," added Bill. "Especially when we're bored."

"Then what in space *are* we to do? The crew's jumpy and I don't blame them."

"We can't turn off our imaginations," said Anthea slowly. "But maybe we could try to fill them with something less scary. Just till we get safely to Obduran."

The bridge was silent while they thought. A knife-edged pendulum suddenly appeared suspended from the ceiling and swung slowly to and fro. Someone on board was reading *The Pit and the Pendulum*.

They all leapt back. The duty officer screamed and punched the alarm bell. Klaxons hooted throughout the ship. The *Orion Queen* lurched and gained speed as someone in engineering boosted the thrusters.

Captain Mirador sprang to the helm. "What in space are you doing down there? Resume normal speed," he yelled. "First Officer, kill the alarm and get that man to sick bay." He caught sight of Anthea and Bill cowering in a corner. "As for you kids . . . Off my bridge. I'm sick of the sight of you."

Bill and Anthea gathered up every book and comic and locked them safely away. Then they looked blankly at each other.

"What'll we do now?" Bill asked.

"We could tell the kids stories, I suppose. D'you know any good ones?"

Bill thought about it and shook his head. "I can't think of anything but videos I've seen. And they're all about haunted houses and homicidal maniacs. Stuff like that."

"Ssh!" Anthea put her hand over his mouth. "Don't even *think* . . ." From the corridor outside there came a horrendous scream.

"I can't stop!" Bill jumped to his feet, his hands to his head. "It's awful. The more I don't think about it, the more I do."

"You've got to try," Anthea begged. "I think the entity is getting stronger."

The klaxon sounded again and the *Orion Queen* shuddered. Natalie and Madeline whimpered and hugged each other.

"Do something," Ollie yelled. "You two are the oldest."

Anthea stared blankly at the box of books that had been the start of all their troubles. Then she dropped to her knees and unlocked it.

"Anthea, are you crazy?"

"It's in here somewhere, I know it is. Ah!" She held up a small brown-backed book. "Now gather round, kids, and listen hard. *The Wind in the Willows* by Kenneth Grahame." She turned to the first page. " 'The Mole had been working very hard all the morning, spring cleaning his little home . . .' "

It worked like a charm. Anthea and Bill took turns reading to the younger kids. When they had finished, they began again at the beginning. There was no more green slime. There were no headless men. The crew became quite fond of Rat and Mole, strolling arm in arm along the starboard gangway. Badger spent his days on the bridge, while Toad was always to be found in the engine room.

The only remaining problem was a vague haunting, a whistling, a pattering, the gleam of eyes — evil, sharp, malicious, and hateful — in the side corridors. It terrified the smaller children, and after a while, even the stoutest crew member became uneasy.

Anthea and Bill looked at each other. "Got it!" exclaimed Bill, and the kids made signs and fastened them to the walls of the haunted corridors. They all read To the Wild Wood and they pointed toward a small, locked storeroom right next to the cargo bay.

As the weeks went by, and the terrors faded from the minds of the smaller children, they dared each other to tiptoe down the port gangway and listen at the storeroom door. They said you could hear, on the other side, the urgent pitter-patter of the weasels and ferrets in the Wild Wood.

That, except for Rat, Mole, and Badger, was the last, the very last, of the haunting of the *Orion Queen*.

• • •

Carole Spray

THE KESWICK VALLEY GHOST

I adapted this from a story told by Professor Robert Cockburn in his office at the University of New Brunswick. Bob heard the story from the people who lived in the house.

Among the many beautiful old homes in the Keswick Valley, there is one house that was abandoned and remained empty for a long time. Nobody would live in it. In fact, many people were afraid to go near it. On dark nights a strange amber glow could be seen moving from window to window in the upper part of the house, and those who saw the ghostly light were convinced that the place was haunted.

The building stood vacant for many years, until one day a young couple came from far away and looked at the old house and decided that they liked it very much. They found much to admire in its unusual structure and in its gracious rooms and in the large expanse of field and forest that surrounded the property. When they discovered that the owner was willing to sell the place at a very low price, nothing could dissuade the young couple from buying it. And when the people of the valley came to warn them that the house was haunted by a ghost, the man and his wife merely laughed. They did not believe in such things.

As soon as the couple moved in they began to paint and make repairs. They put in new plumbing and wiring and they sanded the wooden floors and waxed them. They spent all their money renovating the place. Soon the house looked as splendid as it did when it was first built more than a hundred years before. It was a beautiful house, and the couple were very happy there. Many months went by, and there was no sign of anything that remotely resembled a ghost.

But one day in July, something unusual happened. A small pane of glass in the upstairs window suddenly and inexplicably smashed into thousands of small pieces. The window appeared to have been shattered from the inside. Neither the man nor his wife had been near the window when the pane shattered, and there had not been anyone else in the house at the time. They investigated both the inside of the house and the outside, and in the end, they still could not explain why the window broke the way it did. But after a while, they stopped talking about what had happened and eventually they almost forgot about it.

However, the following year on the very same date,

the glass broke again. It was smashed from the inside. Again, nobody had been near the window when it broke. And for some mysterious reason, the same window continued to break on the same date, year after year. That was the first thing that happened.

Then, a few years after they moved into the house, the wife began to have a dream. She would dream the same dream over and over again. In her dream she saw a man on horseback riding past the house toward the bank of the river. The man was dressed in an old-fashioned uniform. It was the kind of outfit that a British Army officer could have worn a century before. He wore a military jacket that was bottle-green in color, and he had a three-cornered hat decorated with a badge of some sort. His trousers were white and they were tucked into a pair of knee-high, laced moccasins. The man's face was pale and distraught, and in the woman's dream he would always turn to her and declare, "I didn't do it! I didn't do it!"

The wife had this dream several times a year, and the dream recurred so frequently it began to bother her and she became very curious. Who was the figure in her dream? And why was he so distressed?

The couple began to question the people in the valley, and they were told many things. One of the stories they heard appeared to have some connection with the dream.

It seems that at one time the house in which they lived was used as a resting place for soldiers and wayfarers who traveled between Quebec and Fredericton. Travelers could get a meal there and sometimes people stayed overnight. It happened that the paymaster for the British regiment stationed in Fredericton had to make the journey from Quebec City and he had in his possession a large amount of gold, which was to be used to pay the soldiers of the Fredericton battalion. It is likely that he had a number of guards with him for protection, because it was very dangerous to travel the highways alone with so much money. Often people were beaten and robbed for much less than the fortune in gold he was carrying with him.

It was a long and tiresome journey by horseback, so the paymaster and the rest of his company decided to stay the night at the house in the Keswick Valley. Then, in the morning, they would travel the thirty kilometers into Fredericton. But the paymaster never finished his journey. That night he was murdered and the payroll was stolen and nobody knows whether or not the murderer was caught.

After she heard this story, the wife felt fairly certain that the figure in her dream was one of the guards and that he had been wrongly accused of the crime. She thought the words "I didn't do it," which he repeated so often, were perhaps a desperate plea to convince someone of his innocence.

But there was one thing that puzzled the woman. In her dream the road that the man on horseback traveled the side of the house and along the river bank.

he side of the house and along the river bank was

own up in trees and bushes, and there was no sign

road there. Not a trace of one. Finally she and her

sband located some old maps of the area, and they dis-

overed that the original road was exactly where she

dreamed it had been. Both the man and his wife were

strangers to the Keswick Valley, so neither of them could have known about the old road. And yet, in her dream, the wife had seen the landscape as it was more than a hundred years ago when the murder was supposed to have taken place.

About ten years ago an old woman came to the door of the house. She had been absent from the Keswick Valley for forty years, but she had grown up in the house and she asked if she could see it again. The young couple were willing to oblige and they showed her through all the rooms — they took her from the attic at the top of the house to the cellar at the bottom. Just as she was about to leave, the old woman turned to the wife and whispered, "Have you ever seen IT?"

Of course, they had never actually seen anything, and so the wife replied, "No. . . . What do you mean?"

The old woman didn't answer. Instead, she hurried away from the house, and the young couple were puzzled.

But one summer when the wife was upstairs taking a nap at two o'clock in the afternoon, she awoke suddenly and saw a strange shape standing in the doorway. She couldn't tell whether the shape was that of a man or a woman, but it seemed to be an amber color. She decided to go to the door to see who or what it was standing there, but as soon as she got up, the shape disappeared.

Since then, neither the man nor the woman have seen or heard anything else. But right to this day, the wife continues to have the same dream. And the same window pane continues to break regularly on the same date, every year.

• • •

James F. Robinson

FIVE CANDLES ON A COFFIN

In the summer of 1822 Catherine Ryan, at the age of sixty-seven, was well loved by her family and friends and liked and respected by her neighbors in the Ernestown area. Born in Ireland in 1755, she had come to Canada with her first husband, who had served in the British Army under Wolfe at Quebec and later with Jessup's Rangers in the American Revolution. After the death of her first husband, Catherine remarried and came to the Kingston area with her second husband and a growing family in 1784. After her second husband died, she moved her family to a farm in Camden Township. It is there that our story begins.

That fateful summer of 1822 Catherine set out with her fifteen-year-old grandson to pick up supplies in Kingston. At this time there were no highways or roads, only trails, which followed concession lines where possible, with many detours to avoid marshy places. They had to cross streams on crude bridges or by fording as they traveled to Camden East and then eastward to Wilton. They then climbed up the east slope of the valley and headed south to Westbrook. After crossing Collins Creek, they continued east along Woodbine Road to the Five Mile House. The tiresome journey had taken most of the day.

As night was approaching, Catherine and her grandson stopped at the Five Mile House. While Catherine was watering the horses, her grandson went to see about a room for the night. When she had finished, Catherine sat down. Looking around, she saw under the inn shed a coffin on which sat five lighted candles. As she stared at the ominous sight, her grandson returned. Catherine grabbed the reins and told him to get on the wagon. Then she whipped the horses into a gallop and raced down the road. At Waterloo, now Cataraqui Village, they stopped and spent the night. She told her grandson of what she had seen. He had apparently seen nothing.

Early the next day they drove into Kingston. There they completed their business by mid-morning and started back home. When they reached the Five Mile House, they stopped to rest and water the horses. As the horses were drinking a sudden noise startled them. The horses panicked, jackknifed the wagon, and tipped its platform. Catherine was thrown to the ground. A barrel of salt fell off the tilted wagon and crushed her fatally.

They saw to it that she was laid in a coffin under the inn shed and that five lighted candles were placed on top of the coffin lid.

• • •

Paul Yee

SPIRITS OF THE RAILWAY

One summer many, many years ago, heavy flood waters suddenly swept through south China again. Farmer Chu and his family fled to high ground and wept as the rising river drowned their rice crops, their chickens, and their water buffalo.

With his family's food and farm gone, Farmer Chu went to town to look for work. But a thousand other starving peasants were already there. So when he heard there was work across the ocean in the New World, he borrowed some money, bought a ticket, and off he sailed.

Long months passed as his family waited to hear from him. Farmer Chu's wife fell ill from worry and weariness. From her hard board bed she called out her husband's name over and over, until at last her eldest son borrowed money to cross the Pacific in search of his father.

For two months young Chu listened to waves batter the groaning planks of the ship as it crossed the ocean.

For two months he dreaded that he might drown at any minute. For two months he thought of nothing but his father and his family.

Finally he arrived in a busy port city. He asked everywhere for his father, but no one in Chinatown had heard the name. There were thousands of Chinese flung throughout the New World, he was told. Gold miners scrabbled along icy rivers, farmers ploughed the long low valleys, and laborers traveled through towns and forests, from job to job. Who could find one single man in this enormous wilderness?

Young Chu was soon penniless. But he was young and strong, and he feared neither danger nor hard labor. He joined a work gang of thirty Chinese, and a steamer ferried them up a river canyon to build the railway.

When the morning mist lifted, Chu's mouth fell open. On both sides of the rushing river, gray mountains rose like walls to block the sky. The rock face dropped into ragged cliffs that only eagles could ascend and jutted out from cracks where scrawny trees clung. Never before had he seen such towering ranges of dark, raw rock.

The crew pitched their tents and began to work. They hacked at hills with hand-scoops and shovels to level a pathway for the train. Their hammers and chisels chipped boulders into gravel and fill. Their dynamite and drills thrust tunnels deep into the mountain. At night the crew would sit around the campfire chewing tobacco, playing cards, and talking.

From one camp to another the men trekked up the rail line, their food and tools dangling from sturdy shoulder poles. When they met other workers, Chu would run ahead and shout his father's name and ask for news. But the workers just shook their heads grimly.

"Search no more, young man!" one grizzled old worker said. "Don't you know that too many have died here? My own brother was buried alive in a mudslide."

"My uncle was killed in a dynamite blast," muttered another. "No one warned him about the fuse."

The angry memories rose and swirled like smoke among the workers.

"The white boss treats us like mules and dogs!"

"They need a railway to tie this nation together, but they can't afford to pay decent wages."

"What kind of country is this?"

Chu listened, but still he felt certain that his father was alive.

Then winter came and halted all work. Snows buried everything under a heavy blanket of white. The white boss went to town to live in a warm hotel, but Chu and the workers stayed in camp. The men tied potato sacks around their feet and huddled by the fire, while ice storms howled like wolves through the mountains. Chu thought the winter would never end.

When spring finally arrived, the survivors struggled outside and shook the chill from their bones. They dug graves for two workers who had succumbed to sickness. They watched the river surge alive from the melting snow. Work resumed, and Chu began to search again for his father.

Late one afternoon the gang reached a mountain with a half-finished tunnel. As usual, Chu ran up to shout his father's name, but before he could say a word, other workers came running out of the tunnel.

"It's haunted!" they cried. "Watch out! There are ghosts inside!"

"Dark figures slide soundlessly through the rocks!" one man whispered. "We hear heavy footsteps approaching but never arriving. We hear sighs and groans coming from corners where no man stands."

Chu's friends dropped their packs and refused to set up camp. But the white boss rode up on his horse and shook his fist at the men. "No work, no pay!" he shouted. "Now get to work!"

Then he galloped off. The workers squatted on the rocks and looked helplessly at one another. They needed the money badly for food and supplies.

Chu stood up. "What is there to fear?" he cried. "The ghosts have no reason to harm us. There is no reason to be afraid. We have hurt no one."

"Do you want to die?" a man called out.

"I will spend the night inside the tunnel," Chu declared as the men muttered unbelievingly. "Tomorrow we can work."

Chu took his bedroll, a lamp, and food and marched into the mountain. He heard the crunch of his boots and the sound of water dripping. He knelt to light his lamp. Rocks lay in loose piles everywhere, and the shadowy walls closed in on him.

At the end of the tunnel he sat down and ate his food. He closed his eyes and wondered where his father was. He pictured his mother weeping in her bed and heard her voice calling his father's name. He lay down, pulled his blankets close, and eventually he fell asleep.

Chu awoke gasping for breath. Something heavy was pressing down on his chest. He tried to raise his arms, but could not. He clenched his fists and summoned all his strength, but still he was paralyzed. His eyes strained into the darkness, but saw nothing.

Suddenly the pressure eased and Chu groped for the lamp. As the chamber sprang into light, he cried, "What do you want? Who are you?"

Silence greeted him, and then a murmur sounded from behind. Chu spun around and saw a figure in the shadows. He slowly raised the lamp. The flickering light traveled up bloodstained trousers and a mud-encrusted jacket. Then Chu saw his father's face.

"Papa!" he whispered, lunging forward.

"No! Do not come closer!" The figure stopped him. "I am not of your world. Do not embrace me."

Tears rose in Chu's eyes. "So it's true," he choked. "You . . . you have left us. . . ."

His father's voice quivered with rage. "I am gone, but I am not done yet. My son, an accident here killed many men. A fuse exploded before the workers could run. A ton of rock dropped on us and crushed us flat. They buried the whites in a churchyard, but our bodies were thrown into the river, where the current swept us away. We have no final resting place."

Chu fell upon his knees. "What shall I do?"

His father's words filled the tunnel. "Take chopsticks; they shall be our bones. Take straw matting; that can be our flesh. Wrap them together and tie them tightly. Take the bundles to the mountain top high above the nests of eagles, and cover us with soil. Pour tea over our beds. Then we shall sleep in peace."

When Chu looked up, his father had vanished. He stumbled out of the tunnel and blurted the story to his friends. Immediately they prepared the bundles and sent him off with ropes and a shovel to the foot of the cliff, and Chu began to climb.

When he swung himself over the top of the cliff, he was so high up that he thought he could see the distant ocean. He dug the graves deeper than any wild animal could dig, and laid the bundles gently in the earth.

Then Chu brought his fists together above his head and bowed three times. He knelt and touched his forehead to the soil three times. In a loud, clear voice he declared, "Three times I bow, three things I vow. Your pain shall stop now, your sleep shall soothe you now, and I will never forget you. Farewell."

Then, hanging onto a rope looped around a tree, Chu slid slowly back down the cliff. When he reached the bottom, he looked back and saw that the rope had turned into a giant snake that was sliding smoothly up the rock face.

"Good," he smiled to himself. "It will guard the graves well." Then he returned to the camp, where he and his fellow workers lit their lamps and headed into the tunnel. And spirits never again disturbed them, nor the long trains that came later.

• • •

Tim Wynne-Jones

THE CLEARING

The boy stopped at the top of You-And-Me-Pal Hill and kicked off his skis. He leaned against a rock. The sun was high and the glare on the snow hurt his eyes. He hurt everywhere. But at least he was outside again, moving through the windless day, his skis breaking a new trail.

He got his breath back. He couldn't shake the dizziness, but he settled into the middle of it, found somewhere there that wasn't moving. Down the high meadow was Far-Enough Swamp, though he couldn't see it through the cedar and balsam that hugged the reedy shore.

"This is rich land," his dad had said once. "Where else you gonna find a swamp with a fir collar?"

The boy trained his eyes at a break in the trees. If this was a time-travel story, someone would come now. Maybe a Mohawk brave silently tracking a white-tail deer. He was ready. He would jump out at the deer and scare it — herd it — back into the path of the brave's arrow. It was a cold winter. The brave would be thankful. He might take the boy back home to meet his dad and mom.

The boy watched and waited. Nothing.

Rich land — what a joke. Solid granite with a rind of dirt only Pollyanna could call soil. Farmers had once tried to cultivate this area. Snow-rounded pyramids of rocks along the cedar fence lines testified to their efforts; those and straggly apple orchards gone wild. But these meadows had been turned over to the hardier grasses; to juniper and thorn and prickly ash; to the fir trees that ringed Far-Enough Swamp.

The boy took a deep breath of bright, cold air. It was −10°C, but he took off his gloves. They were wet inside with sweat, like the sheets of the bed he had left behind, clammy and constricting.

Where was his time-travel connection? In those stories the hero was always lonely, and he was lonely. The kid in a time-travel story was usually sick, too, and he was sick. For how long now, he didn't care to recall.

He started to shiver. Then he slipped back into his skis and shooshed down the meadow toward the gap in the trees that led to the swamp.

On the swamp there were many tracks: brush wolf and fox and rabbit. No humans. He followed the path of two wolves who seemed to be going more or less his way.

There was a wire fence property line right through the middle of the swamp. He climbed over it without taking off his skis. He imagined himself making an escape. He pushed himself hard, ducking invisible enemy fire, until the fence and his imaginary enemy were lost to view around a bend in the meandering waterway. Deeper and deeper he escaped into the silent forest, a graveyard of gray stumps and the spiny skeletons of trees.

He was trespassing now. This was Ken Axelrod's land and, after crossing the dyke, the Starkweathers, the Beresfords, the Strongs, the Frosts. But after that, he couldn't say anymore where he was. There were no signs of civilization out here and, in his dizziness, the sun was no help — it seemed lost itself. The only thing he knew for sure was that he was heading away, his sick bed slipping farther and farther behind.

At last he saw something in the distance that was not dead, not stumps. A hockey rink in a clearing. Rag-tag nets; sticks, broken or intact, stuck in the snowbank like a rickety fence; a bench carved out of ice with an old pine plank on top. A frozen toque.

Coming to the rink, the boy slipped out of his skis. He sat on the bench. He noticed the snow shovels. Suddenly, sick and tired as he was, an idea started ticking over in him.

There was three or four centimeters of fresh snow on the rink. The boy pushed at the snow with his foot; it flew up like so many feathers. He started to shovel. The joke of it flowed like fresh blood to his aching muscles. He shoveled like a boy possessed. He laughed a little to himself. He whistled.

Then, just as suddenly, he stopped. Looking up, he saw someone in the trees at the swamp's edge staring at him. He felt cold all over.

"Hey," the boy on the ridge called to him. "Hi."

Shaking, he dropped the shovel and ran for his skis. He fumbled with his binding. There was no such thing as time travel. There was only wishful thinking. This should not have happened.

The boy was coming. "It's all right," he cried.

But it wasn't all right. The intruder was stomping, sliding down the slope of the woods to the shoreline.

The skier turned himself toward home. His tips crossed and he fell over hard, then clambered to his feet again.

"Wait," the intruder cried. "Don't go."

The skier pushed himself off, digging his ski pole tips through the downy snow into the ice itself. Heaving himself homeward, following his tracks.

"Hey, I can help," yelled the intruder, coming nearer, crossing the ice, slipping, recovering.

But the skier was off. The other boy would never catch him now.

"Come again," the intruder called after him.

Ben watched until the skier was out of sight. He took over shoveling where the other boy had left off, stopping often and staring out across the swamp. The sun was sitting low behind the hills, casting long blue shadows. Sometimes he fancied he saw the boy far off, a lean shadow disentangling itself from those of dead trees.

The wind picked up. Already the ski tracks were sifting over. Ben pushed the snow around in a desultory way. After a while he heard his father coming. He put his shoulder down and heaved snow manfully.

"Yowzers!" said his father, with enough surprise in his voice that Ben laughed inside. "Good work, Ben."

"Ah, it was nothing," said Ben, huffing it up a bit.

"Pretty industrious," said his father. Ben thanked him. Out of the corner of his eye he caught his father scratching his head. "I came to give you a hand."

Ben stopped, sucked in a bucketful of frosty air. "I can handle it, Dad," he said, leaning on his shovel.

His father waited a minute more while Ben went on shoveling.

"I'm sorry about the fight," said his father. Ben scraped his shovel over the ice.

"That's OK," he mumbled, without turning around.

"It's just that . . ." his father began, ". . . sometimes it's as if you didn't really move out here with us at all."

That's dumb! Ben wanted to shout. Where am I? Back home in the city? What choice does a twelve-year-old have but to be wherever his parents take him! But he didn't say a thing, because it would come out wrong and ungrateful and the argument would start all over again. And that would ruin the wonderful joke of this magically cleared rink.

After some more minutes his father said, "It'll be dark soon," and he headed back toward the woods, the path, the house. When he was out of sight, Ben surveyed what was left of the smooth blanket of snow on the ice and went to work with a vengeance. It was some creative shoveling he did. Then he went home hungry for supper and ready to make up properly.

In the snow still left on the rink, he had written

COME AGAIN

Before the school bus the next morning he ran down from the house to check. His message was mostly gone. The rink was clear, but it appeared to be the work of the wind.

Over the next few days it warmed up. Then it froze. Then it snowed a whole night. Then the sun shone hot. It was a winter spell set on killing a swamp skating rink. But Ben's father wasn't the kind of man who gave up on a pet project easily. He and Ben tried to keep the surface smooth, mostly for Ben's sisters. Ben liked hockey, but he hadn't really gotten to know anyone much since they'd moved to the valley, and playing hockey by yourself was — well, you could only score the winning goal in the final game of the Stanley Cup so many times before the thrill wore off. But whether he used the rink or not, he and his father would come down, often in the chill of the night, and fill buckets with water from a hole to spread as best they could — "Smoother, Ben, smoother" — under the icy moon.

Ben would always have his eye open for the stranger. He would look up suddenly across the swamp.

"Did you hear that?" he would say.

"You're a jumpy customer," his father would answer, not listening long enough or hard enough, shaking his head and chuckling to himself.

Ben asked on the school bus who the kid might be. It gave him something to talk about.

The weather heated up unseasonably. The top of the rink in the clearing thawed, then froze again from the top down, leaving a sandwich of water between the new ice and the thick gray ice below.

That was the first time Ben saw mayfly wrigglers. The water nymphs swam up through cracks in the thick ice and got themselves stuck in the watery sandwich. Having escaped from the winter dark at the bottom of the pond, they swam like crazy black writing in the sunlight. They were stuck there. They were not alone. Ben saw a black splotch under the new ice. He was just wondering how a puck had got there when the splotch moved.

"Look at this!" he cried.

"Bullfrog tadpole," said his dad. "It'll die there, unless it finds its way back down. Shouldn't have been so nosy."

Ben wanted to watch it, but the new ice wasn't very thick, and his father didn't want him to go through and wreck the surface. They went up for dinner with the tadpole, big as a puck, in Ben's head. It swam around just under his skull, wanting out.

That night the moon was full again. And whether it was the moon or the trapped tadpole or just life, Ben and his folks got into another fight.

Ben wasn't ever sure how these things happened. He was usually reading an Archie comic at the time or re-arranging his baseball card collection. The argument was always over something he had said or hadn't done or had implied or had complained about.

In his room, with a slammed door separating him from the family, Ben opened his journal to the last page where he kept his fight record.

<u>Mom</u>   <u>Dad</u>
X X X X X X   X X X X X X X X

He added a new X to Mom's column. She was catching up to Dad. He could still hear her pounding about downstairs, her voice raised for him to hear, door or no door.

He never got hit, but the words were big and noisy, like God yelling at Moses: words that blew your ears off.

Reaching for his baseball dictionary, Ben flipped to "earned run average."

earned run average n. (ERA) A pitcher's statistics representing the average number of runs legitimately scored from his deliveries per full nine-inning game (27 outs).

He tried to figure out his earned fight average n. (EFA). Earned — how did you determine that? What was average? What made a fight legitimate? Did he ever win any? Ben messed with his pen on some scrap paper while his heart turned around in his chest like a dog looking for some place to settle down. Then he started to draw: a guy sliding into second just under the ball; just under the sweeping hand of the second baseman. Safe. When spring started again, there would be baseball. If he could just make it through this endless winter to baseball. . . .

He turned the pages in the journal to the entry he had written about the Phantom Shoveler. He had painted a little comic strip in watercolors. In the picture Ben cried after the shoveler, "Come back, come back, I've still got the driveway to do!" Now he noticed the date on the page. It had been the day of the last full moon.

His dad suddenly opened the door, and Ben slammed the journal shut. Later he wasn't quite sure why the apology he tried to make resulted in another yelling match and another slammed door. He sat on his bed for a long time, trying to figure out whether this was actually a new fight for which he should reward his father with an X, raising his EFA, or whether this was just the same fight he had been having with his mom and into which his dad had entered, kind of like a reliever in the late innings of a game.

Nobody came to kiss him goodnight. He didn't change into his pajamas. He didn't turn out his light. He stomped, boiling mad, downstairs and made himself some toast just after his parents had put the girls to bed. He made several trips to the bathroom. In short, he gave them every opportunity to crab at him some more, so that he could stumble through a real apology. Then everyone could make up and get the whole thing out of the way, and he could get to sleep. Instead, they left him to stew in his own juices.

Finally he heard them in the bathroom preparing for bed. Surely now they would notice his light. The door was wide open.

They didn't. He heard them turn out their own lights without so much as looking in on him.

They were treating him as if he were gone. As if maybe they had left him back in the city.

Ben flicked out his own bedside light and sat, arms crossed tight on his chest, breathing heavily in the dark. But it was not really dark; there was a full moon. It was almost bright enough to read by. Bright enough to leave by.

He was as quiet as a mouse until he was out of the house and then he slammed the door good and loud. Just one more slammed door in a night of slammed doors.

He was halfway to the clearing before he realized where he was heading. He had never been out in the woods so late — not alone, at least. Once the family had skated under the full moon with a bunch of neighbors, and even his sisters had stayed up until almost midnight. But on that occasion the bright night had been filled with chatter and hot chocolate, and he had not heard the noise the night makes all on its own. In the dead of winter, that noise is Silence.

Silence was something he had never heard in the city. It was a Silence to fill the wildness of the eastern forest; a Silence as tall as the pines, as wide and as deep as the swampland. It filled him with an urgent longing.

He stood among the trees on the shore looking out at the shining rink. He waited for his father to come tromping through the brush after him. "Ben, Ben, this is ridiculous!" Then he could hurl himself at his father's chest and into his arms. But his father didn't come, and the Silence grew around him.

Then, because he had to do something to occupy his runaway mind, he slithered down the snowy bank to the swamp and walked quickly out across the clearing to the rink. There was a wind out there he had not felt in the shelter of the trees. It was a sound, anyway, almost soothing.

It took some time to locate the huge tadpole. On his knees to better spread out his weight, Ben watched it for several moments fearing that it was already dead, perhaps frozen into place, for the night had turned cold. Then it moved, squirming slowly but too stupid cold to look for the hole through which it had slipped into this place between places.

"Yes!" said Ben, and in a flash he was on his feet again and searching for his father's axe. He brought the axe down hard on the new ice — once, twice, three times — before finally cracking it. That woke the tadpole up!

"It's for your own good," said Ben.

The tadpole didn't swim far. It was trapped every which way, in the last pool of unfrozen water, a pool no more than a meter in diameter.

Ben whacked some more. Each whack sounded like a gunshot. Finally, with one last, mighty swing — Splat! — water sprayed up at him. He had broken through. He chipped away the chunks of surface ice, brought over the coffee can that his father used as a small bucket, and attempted to catch the frantic prisoner. He had made several dives at it, and his cuffs were getting pretty wet, when someone spoke.

"You gonna destroy the whole rink?"

For one wild, midnight second, Ben thought it was the tadpole. Then he swung around so fast that the bottom half of him slid into the pond.

There, just behind him, stood the phantom skier.

"The rink," said the boy. "You destroying it?"

"No," said Ben. "There's this tadpole." He clambered up, shaking his cold, damp leg to get some of the water off it. The boy approached him cautiously. Ben backed off a little. The boy looked into the hole. Ben saw the sweat stand out on his cheek and forehead, saw that he was shivering badly.

The stranger bent down. "Can you catch him?" he said.

Ben dropped to his wet knees beside the boy and picked up the coffee can. The stranger leaned back on his haunches, watching as Ben lowered the can into the shallow icy pond, quite suddenly an expert at the moonlight capturing of trapped tadpoles. In one deft swoop he swooshed the can out of the pond, triumphant. The two boys peered into it together and then ventured to look at each other.

"Come on," said Ben. He led the other boy to the hole his father kept open on the edge of the rink in order to draw water from the swamp below. It was covered with a bucket. "Here you go," said Ben, emptying the can into the hole. With a flip of its tail the creature was gone. The two boys watched the darkness for a moment.

"In a cartoon," said Ben, "the tadpole would come to the surface and wink or something."

"Or there would be a bubble," said the boy, "and when you popped it the word 'thanks' would come floating out."

They smiled at each other. It was only a fleeting

smile. Each of them had things on his mind. The stranger looked back to the axe hole in the rink.

"I'll have some explaining to do," said Ben. "But I think my dad will understand."

"You took some initiative," said the boy, the tail of a smile reappearing on his pale face.

"Right," said Ben. "I was industrious." They both laughed. Then, because he couldn't hold it any longer, Ben said, "Who are you?"

It was exactly the wrong thing to say. The boy's face seemed troubled again. He looked back at the hole in the rink and then at the open hole in front of them and then all around, as if he were looking for something, some way to explain.

"I didn't mean to be rude," said Ben. But it was already too late. The boy stood up, tall and thin — too thin. Head down, he went for his skis. "Wait," said Ben, desperate now, for he was losing people all over the place tonight.

"I can't stay," said the boy.

"Then I'll come with you," said Ben, following him, staying close enough to touch the boy's elbow.

"You can't," said the boy, pulling his arm out of reach. He clipped on his skis.

"Why not?" said Ben.

The boy was breathing hard. He started moving,

finding his tracks in the snow. "You won't be able to keep up," he called over his shoulder.

Ben started after the boy on foot. "Just watch me," he shouted, breaking into a tight and cautious run. "I can't go home. Wait up."

Across the moonlit swamp he pursued the skier, falling farther and farther behind. "I'll get lost," he yelled. "And it'll be your fault!"

"Go home," the boy called back at him.

It started to snow, one more curtain between Ben and home and between Ben and the boy, now almost out of sight. But Ben wasn't going to let go of him. He followed the tracks. How hard it was to move on this land without skis. His legs were city legs: pavement hard and strong, but he could not keep his footing on the snow-covered swamp. He would break through the crust here, slip out on the ice there. But he kept going.

At one point the ski trail joined up with the tracks of a pair of coyotes — brush wolves they called them around here. Ben faltered in his stride.

"Please!" he called out across the swamp. "I don't want to be somebody's dinner."

"Go home."

Then, finally, the tracks came to a fence, and not far beyond that headed toward the shoreline, the woods. In the fringe of trees there was no wind and Ben paused for a moment to catch his breath. He looked back across the swamp. The snow fell quietly. Already it had laid fine tissue in his footsteps. How much longer would there be a path to follow home?

Then, behind him, back in the direction he had come from, the coyotes howled. It was a mad yip, yip, yipping. The sound zinged through him. He was not the only crazy one on the prowl tonight. It was the moon they wanted, not him, he told himself, but the sound was enough to send him quickly on his way, after the boy.

At the top of the meadow he stopped at a rocky outcropping. Looking down the other side, he thought he saw a striding shadow slip into the woods. "Yes!" He tore off in pursuit. Sinking into the deep drifts of the meadow, scratching himself in the prickly ash, pressed on by the baying coyotes, following tracks that grew fainter and fainter under the snow-beclouded moon.

He emerged at last from an old logging road at a small, neat cottage with the lights still on. It was like something from a fairy tale, with him as the miserable, poor straggler. Unable to move another step, breathing heavily, soaked with sweat, and numb where the icy water of his tadpole rescue mission had soaked through his jeans, he leaned against a tree. He caught his breath and watched the uncurtained windows of the cottage. He could make out a woman reading by a fire. No one else.

Ben gathered up what was left of his shredded

courage and marched up to the door. When he was close enough, he checked the walls to make sure they were not gingerbread.

He had no idea what he was going to say. His mind was muzzy with the cold and a buzzing tiredness of limb and spirit he had never experienced before. He would have to say something, he told himself, and though words would not form in his head, he knocked again and again. Then the woman was at the door, opening it in a hurry, keeping back a barking, slathering golden retriever with her foot, and all Ben could think to say was "I'd like to phone my mom, please."

She took him in. The dog bounced on him. A man appeared in his undershirt and cleared a place by the fire. Tea came, and blankets. The man made a joke about what Ben's chattering teeth were saying in Morse code, and by then Ben could actually laugh a little, though he had no right to laugh or even to be alive, he reckoned, all things considered. He told them about the coyotes. They had heard them too.

The woman got his phone number and talked to his mom. She turned to him. "She's on her way."

Then Ben asked if a boy lived there.

"No," said the woman, shaking her head. "A daughter off at college. No boy." So he didn't tell them about the skier.

It was Ben's dad who came because the coyotes had

woken up both the girls with full-moon nightmares, and Mom was feeding them full-moon carrot cake and hot milk.

"So you'll be coming home to a party," his father said, squeezing him tightly. No one asked any questions. Ben didn't try to explain. Dad had met the couple, the Robbs, at some valley shindig. He couldn't thank them enough.

"Ah, heck," said Mr. Robb. "It kind of livens up a dull evening." And then it was time for Ben to change into the warm clothes his father had brought along and head home.

At the front door Ben noticed a pair of skis. They were leaning in the corner of the mud room. They were just like the ones the boy had worn. But they weren't wet at all. The woman noticed him looking at them, and she got a frown on her face, which made Ben feel bad. He concentrated on putting on his boots. His hands were shaking badly.

They were climbing into the car and Dad was tucking him into the passenger seat like a little kid when the door of the cottage reopened and Mrs. Robb called out to Ben's father. He closed Ben's door and went back to the house. Ben watched them talking through the oval window of the door. Then, amazed, he saw the woman handing the skis to his father. Meanwhile, Mr. Robb opened a closet and emerged with ski boots and poles. Then it was goodbye all over again and Dad was making his way to the car laden down with this mysterious treasure. The skis wouldn't fit in the trunk so they had to be shoved into the back seat with the tips hanging over Ben's shoulder.

"They're for you," said his father with a catch in his voice. "Make getting around out here a whole lot easier." He didn't say anything about running away.

And he didn't say any more just then. Ben looked at him in the dashboard light and saw that he was choked up about something.

"It was the last thing they had left of their own son," his father said at last. There was a long pause. Snow fell. Ben kept his eyes on the road.

"It's been five years."

They turned onto a now familiar road.

"He was your age."

Neighbors' mailboxes glided by: the Beresfords, Strongs, Frosts.

"They wanted me to thank you."

Thank him? Ben was puzzled. They pulled into the driveway and stopped the car and had a big shaky hug together. Over his father's shoulder, Ben could see his mom in the kitchen, the girls sitting in their nighties. He wanted to get in and be a part of it.

Ben and his dad climbed out of the car wrestling the skis out with them.

"They just couldn't seem to let him go," said his father.

And far away the coyotes started yip, yip, yipping at the moon.

• • •

Andrew MacFarlane

THE MACKENZIE HOMESTEAD

William Lyon Mackenzie was the leader of the 1837 Rebellion in Upper Canada. Many people who have stayed in his house have talked about hauntings. This tale, told to Andrew Mac-Farlane by Charles Edmunds, is one of the most astonishing.

Certain happenings during the three years and eight months my wife and I served as caretakers of the Mackenzie Homestead have convinced me that there is something peculiar about the place.

On one occasion my wife and I were sleeping in the upstairs bedroom. She woke me up in the middle of the night and said that she had seen a man standing beside her bed.

My wife, to my certain knowledge, knew nothing of Mackenzie or his history. All of the pictures in the homestead show Mackenzie as a man with hair on his head. The man my wife saw and described to me was completely bald with side whiskers. I had read about Mackenzie. And I know that the man she described to me was Mackenzie. He wore a wig to cover his baldness. But she did not know this.

On another occasion, just after we moved in, my two grandchildren, Susan (then aged four) and Ronnie (then aged three), went from the upstairs bedroom down to the second-floor bathroom at night.

A few minutes later there were terrific screams. I went down and they were both huddled in the bathroom, terrified. They said there was a lady in the bathroom. I asked where she was now and they said she just disappeared.

On another night my wife woke up screaming. She said: "There was a small man standing over my bed." She described Mackenzie.

Another night a woman came up to the bed and looked at my missus. She was a little woman, about my wife's height. My wife said: "Dear — there was a woman here." I told her she was dreaming.

Another night my wife woke up and woke me. She was upset. She said the lady had hit her. There were three red welts on the left side of her face. They were like finger marks. The next day her eye was bloodshot. Then it turned black and blue. Something hit her. It wasn't me. And I don't think she could have done it herself. And there wasn't anyone else in the house.

On another occasion something peculiar happened with some flowers we had in pots on a window ledge inside the house. This was in winter and we had the geraniums inside. We watered the plants twice a week on Sundays and Wednesdays.

On a Saturday morning we found that they had all been watered, although we hadn't done it. There was water spilled all over the plants and the saucers they were standing in were full. There was mud on the curtains, and holes in the earth as if someone had poked their fingers in the earth. There was water on the dressing-table. Neither of us had watered the plants, and neither had anyone else.

We often heard footsteps on the stairs. Thumping footsteps like someone with heavy boots on. This happened frequently when there was no one in the house but us, when we were sitting together upstairs.

• • •

Hazel Boswell

THE WHITE OWL

I t was a still day late in September. The maples were
glowing scarlet and gold; the plowing had been
done, and the fields lay bare and brown under the
silver-gray sky. Madame Blais sat on an upturned box
on the narrow gallery that ran the length of the summer
kitchen. She was plaiting long strings of red onions to
hang in the attic for the winter. The little gallery was
heaped with vegetables: great golden-yellow squashes,
green pumpkins, creamy brown turnips, and great piles
of green cabbages and glossy red carrots.

It was a good day for work. Her husband and Joseph,
her eldest boy, together with their neighbor, Exdras
Boulay, had gone off to repair the old sugar *cabane*. Her
sister's fiancé, Felix Leroy, who had come up from the
States for a holiday, had gone with them. Not to work.
He despised that sort of work, for he was a factory hand
in the United States and, as he said, "made more money
in a week than he would make in a month working on

the land." The older children were off at school; the little ones, Gaetané, Jean-Paul, and Marie-Ange, were playing happily with old "Puppay." Me'Mère was spinning in the kitchen, keeping an eye on P'tit Charles who was sleeping peacefully in his cradle. Madame worked happily. She didn't often get such a good day for work. Her mind was turning in a placid, peaceful circle, "Que tous s'adone bien aujourd-hui."

Suddenly the peace was broken. Puppay had begun to bark furiously; then the barking changed to joyful yapping. The children were shouting too. Madame turned on her box and looked out to where they had been playing, but they had left their game and were racing off across the field. As her eye followed them on the far side of the field she saw her husband, Joseph, and Exdras Boulay coming out of the wood by the road to the old sugar *cabane*.

Me'Mère had heard the noise too and had come to the door. "What is it?" she asked. "Un Jerusalem?"

"No," answered Madame, "it's the men coming home, and it's not yet four. Something must have happened."

She watched the men anxiously as they crossed the field. She noticed that Felix wasn't with them. As they came up to the house she called out, "What has happened?"

No one answered her; the men tramped on in silence. When they got to the house, her husband sat down on the step of the gallery and began taking off his *bottes-*

sauvages. The other two and the children stood watching him.

"Where is Felix?" asked Madame.

"He wouldn't come with us."

"Why did you leave so early?"

Again there was silence; then her husband said, "We saw the white owl, Le Hibou Blanc."

"You saw him?"

"Yes," answered her husband, "that's why we came home."

"Why didn't Felix come with you?"

"He said it was all nonsense. Old men's stories."

"You should have made him come with you," said Me'Mère. "You can't remember the last time Le Hibou Blanc came. But I can. It was just two years after I was married. Bonté Lemay was like Felix, he didn't believe. He stayed on plowing when the others left. The horse got scared and ran away. Bonté's arm was caught in the reins and he was dragged after the plow. His head struck a stone and he was dead when they found him. His poor mother. How she cried. One doesn't make fun of Le Hibou Blanc."

The noise had wakened P'tit Charles and he began to cry. Madame went in to the kitchen and picked him up. She felt to see if he was wet; and then sat down by the stove, and began to feed him. The men came in too and sat around in the kitchen.

"Do you think Felix will have the sense to come home?" asked Madame.

Joseph shook his head and spat skillfully into the brown earthenware spittoon. "No fear," he answered. "He says in the States they have more sense than to believe all those old stories."

"If Felix stays on in the woods, harm will certainly come to him," said Me'Mère. "I tell you Le Hibou Blanc always brings disaster."

"Why don't you go and speak to the *curé?*" said Madame Blais.

"He's away at Rimouski for a retreat," answered Exdras. "I saw his housekeeper, Philomène, yesterday, and she told me. They had sent for him to bring the last rites to old Audet Lemay who was dying, but he was away and they had to send for the *curé* of St. Anselem instead."

"Well, it's time to get the cows," said Monsieur Blais. "Go along and get them, Joseph."

Joseph got up and went out. The children and Puppay joined him.

Me'Mère went back to her spinning. Madame Blais put P'tit Charles back in his cradle, then went off to milk the cows. There were ten cows to milk. Her husband and Joseph did the milking with her and up to a year before Me'Mère had always helped too. The autumn evenings close in quickly in the north. By the time the cows were milked and supper finished, the clear cold green evening had swept up over the sky; the stars were out, and the little silver crescent of the moon had risen over the maple wood. Joseph was sitting out on the step of the little gallery, his eyes fastened on the break in the maple wood that marked the road leading to the sugar *cabane*. Every now and then his father went out and joined him. They were both watching for Felix.

As the kitchen clock began to strike eight Madame put down her work. "It's time for the rosary," she said. "Tell Joseph to come in." Her husband opened the door and called to Joseph. He came in, followed by Puppay.

The family pulled their chairs up round the stove, for the evenings were beginning to be chilly, and it was cold away from the stove.

Me'Mère began the rosary: "Je crois en Dieu, le Père tout-puissant. . . ." The quiet murmur of their voices filled the kitchen.

When the rosary was said, Madame sent the children off to bed. Then she went to the salon and got a *cierge bénit*, lit it, and put it in the kitchen window. "May God have pity on him," she said. Then she picked up P'tit Charles and went off to bed with her husband, while Me'Mère went to her little room next to the salon.

It was bright and cold the next day, and the ground was covered with white hoarfrost.

Joseph was the first to speak of Felix. "He may have gone and slept with one of the neighbors," he said.

141

"If he did, he'd be back by now," answered his father.

They were still eating their breakfast when Exdras Boulay came into the kitchen. "Felix hasn't come back?" he asked.

Before anyone could answer, the door opened and two other neighbors came in. The news of Felix and Le Hibou Blanc had already spread along the road. Soon there were eight men and boys in the kitchen and half a dozen excited children.

The men sat round in the kitchen smoking. Old Alphonse Ouellet did most of the talking. He was always the leader in the parish.

"We'll have to go and find him," he said.

"It's too bad the *curé* isn't here to come with us. Well, we might as well start off now. Bring your rosary with you," he told Monsieur Blais.

Madame Blais and Me'Mère and a group of the children stood on the kitchen gallery watching the men as they tramped off along the rough track to the maple wood.

"May God have them in His care," said Madame.

"And may He have pity on Felix," added Me'Mère, and she crossed herself.

In the maple wood the ground was still covered with frost. Every little hummock of fallen leaves was white with it, and the puddles along the track were frozen solid. The men walked in silence. A secret fear gripped each one of them that they might suddenly see Le Hibou Blanc perched on some old stump, or one of the snow-covered hummocks. A few hundred meters from the sugar *cabane* they found Felix. He was lying on his back. His red shirt looked at first like a patch of maple leaves lying in the hoarfrost. A great birch had fallen across his chest, pinning him to the ground. One of his hands was grasping a curl of the bark — his last mad effort to try and free himself.

The men stood round staring down at him, the immense silence of the woods surrounding them. Then from far away in the distance came a thin whinnying note, the shrill triumphant cry of Le Hibou Blanc.

• • •

Jean Little

WITHOUT BETH

efore the twins were born, their parents had an argument.

"If it's a girl, I want to name her Elizabeth, after you," their father said.

"Let's not," their mother said. "Elizabeth the Second! It would sound ridiculous."

When the children turned out to be twin daughters, their father was inspired. "How about Eliza and Beth?"

Their mother gave in.

Beth was the younger twin by nine minutes, but that was the only time she let Eliza get ahead of her. Eliza didn't mind. She liked following Beth. Beth made friends for both of them. Beth chose which game they would play.

"Hide-and-seek," she'd call out.

"Good," Eliza would call back. "Beth's it."

Beth named their guinea pigs and their dolls. Their favorite dolls were Christmas presents from Great-aunt Emerald the year they were nine. They too were identical, but Aunt Emerald had dressed one in red and the other in green.

"How about Holly and Ivy?" Beth suggested.

"Perfect," agreed Eliza. "Mine's Holly."

Beth was the twin most people remembered, even though the girls looked so alike. They were small for their age, with taffy-colored hair and wide gray-green eyes and one dimple each.

"Eliza, you're just as smart and pretty as your sister," her anxious parents told her.

"I know," said Eliza. "Stop worrying. I could get along fine without Beth if I had to."

As she said the words, a cold finger of fear touched her. Without Beth. She could not bear to think about her life without her twin. But why should she? They had years to go before they would be grown-ups, and even then, they could arrange to be near each other.

Eliza liked Beth's games and names. She truly wanted to be the lady-in-waiting and the squire and the enemy, and every so often, the loyal hound. She didn't even mind being Beth's stand-in, year after year, at school plays and pageants because it meant she had all the fun of coming to rehearsals with Mrs. Paganini without ever having to play the parts on stage. She quaked at the thought of actually speaking lines in front of a live audience.

"It's a good thing I'm healthy, Eliza," Beth teased when they were in grade seven. "Maybe someday I'll get sick just to see what you'll do."

"Don't," Eliza said, shivering. "Don't get sick."

The play that year was a comedy about a girl in the olden days who decided to cook an elaborate New Year's dinner for her large family and assorted guests and did everything wrong. Eliza knew all the lines by the second day. She was better at memorizing than her sister was.

With astonishment, she watched Beth clowning on stage. The play was not all that good, yet Beth made the mediocre script sparkle. Soon Eliza was chuckling, and at the sentimental finish, she was blinking back tears.

Someday Beth will be a famous actress, she thought. Mrs. Paganini agreed with her.

"This year," she announced, "we're giving two performances. Beth is so good in the main role and people loved her in last year's play. We'll sell tickets and there will be reserved seats. We can donate the money to famine relief."

Everyone practiced harder than ever. Eliza and Beth were so busy they almost forgot to buy tickets for the family. As it was, they could only get three in one row and one directly behind.

"I can sit there," Eliza said. She was excited about seeing the play no matter where she sat.

"You'll need new dresses," their mother said. She bought them scarlet jumpers and white silk blouses. They wore them to Great-aunt Emerald's Christmas party. Aunt Emerald gave Beth a good-luck present. It was a tiny gold star. Beth laughed and pinned it on.

"Is she really a star?" one of their little cousins asked.

"Don't answer that," Beth said. "It might be unlucky to talk about it ahead of time."

"But stars are lucky," the little boy said. "It'll bring good luck to the person who has it, won't it, Aunt Emerald?"

"That was my intention," his great-aunt said.

It did not bring good luck to Beth. She seemed fine all the next day until suppertime. Then she complained of a bad headache and stiffness in her neck. Soon she was running a high fever. At nine o'clock the doctor came. Ten minutes later an ambulance was at the door. Beth was driven away with sirens screaming. Her voice tight and scared, Mum phoned Aunt Emerald. She gave Eliza a quick hug, then she and Dad left for the hospital too. Eliza longed to go with them, but she didn't dare ask.

Aunt Emerald came at once by taxi. Eliza wanted to stay up, but Aunt Emerald fussed over her so that she finally went to her room. Her's and Beth's.

She got into bed, but she couldn't stay there. She prowled around the room, picking up cassette tapes and books she loved and putting them down again. Even though she did her best to keep her back turned, she kept seeing Beth's empty bed.

Finally she grew so weary that she collapsed at the foot of her own bed and dozed. But even half-asleep, she knew, deep inside herself, that Beth was leaving her. Her father came, at last, to tell her that her sister had died. Meningitis. It was a word that would make her shiver even when she was an old lady. At that moment, however, Eliza hardly heard what her father was saying. She was desperately pushing away the very idea of going on without Beth.

"I can't," she whispered. "I don't know how."

"I know," said her father, but he could not really know. Beth was not his twin.

Nobody thought of the school play that day, unless it was Mrs. Paganini. She waited a couple of days, then she came to Eliza's parents. She left it to them to ask Eliza.

"It's the costume partly," Eliza's mother said. "It's an old-fashioned Victorian dress, as you know. Beth was smaller than the others. It would fit you, but it can't be made big enough for anyone else. And Mrs. Paganini says you know all the lines. The part is too long for anyone else to memorize in time. It's up to you, dear. Nobody will blame you if you don't do it, but they have advertised and opening night is sold out. The money . . ."

"I know about the money," Eliza said dully.

She couldn't be Beth. She would make a mess of it. There wasn't even time for her to be in a proper rehearsal. If it weren't for the hungry children, and if the other kids hadn't been practicing so hard . . .

It was time to get dressed before Eliza noticed that her mother had taken away all of Beth's dresses. Or thought she had. When Eliza slid the red jumper over her head and looked in the mirror, she saw, pinned to the front of it, a small gold star.

Her hand reached up and closed on the tiny brooch. Her eyes stung with tears. Then, with trembling fingers, she unfastened it. She was not a star. She knew it already and soon everyone else would too.

Yet, she did not put the pin in her jewel case or throw it out. She slipped it into her pocket. There was a chance, a small chance, that it would help her get through.

The family drove to the school.

"Would you like me to come with you and help you dress?" Mum asked gently. Eliza shook her head. She could not trust her voice. She walked around to the dressing room feeling like a wind-up toy. She answered politely whenever anyone said, "Hi, Eliza." Hardly anyone did. Kids sent her scared glances instead. She put on the long, blue gingham dress, and over it, the frilly pinafore. There seemed to be a million tiny buttons, and before she was through, every one of them was slippery with sweat. At the last moment she took the tiny pin out of her jumper and slid it into the apron pocket. She was as ready as she could be. She wondered what would happen if she threw up on stage.

Mrs. Paganini took Eliza's cold hand and squeezed it. "This way, darling," she said, looking as though she were about to burst into tears.

Eliza took a deep breath and went on stage.

"Are you all set?" the teacher asked huskily.

Eliza nodded, then she walked over to the curtains and parted them slightly. Her right hand dropped to the apron pocket and touched the star. Behind her, Mrs. Paganini blew her nose. But Eliza did not hear her. She was staring through the narrow slit at the rows of people. There were her parents and Great-aunt Emerald. And in Eliza's empty seat, just behind them, sat her sister, Beth.

"It isn't," Eliza breathed, and rubbed her eyes. Beth was still there. She had on a scarlet jumper and a white silk blouse. She was smiling straight at her sister. And as Eliza stared, Beth gave the little salute that, between the two of them, had always meant, "Whatever happens, I'm with you."

"Mrs. Paganini," Eliza said hoarsely. "Come and look at the people."

"I know, I know," the teacher gushed. "It's a full house." She took Eliza's place, peered out at the audience, and smiled broadly. "They're all rooting for you, sweetheart," she said, turning to pat Eliza's arm. Then she headed for the wings, calling over her shoulder, "Break a leg, honey. Curtain in two minutes."

Eliza laughed softly. She did not look to see if Beth was still there. She moved to the table on stage and took her place, pulling the thick cookbook that was her prop toward her. She pushed back her hair as the curtains parted and blew out a loud, thoroughly exasperated sigh.

The audience laughed before she had said a word.

Her family was thunderstruck. This vivid girl couldn't be their quiet Eliza. Even though everyone in the auditorium knew about Beth's death, Eliza kept them chuckling. She played it almost as her sister would have done, but two or three times, she did something Beth would never have thought of. Every time she did, laughter rang out. Until the final moment. Then she had them in tears.

Eliza got a standing ovation. Smiling and bowing, she knew she had earned it. It was not Beth this time, but Eliza on her own — with Beth watching. Life still felt gray and empty, and Eliza knew there was a long lonely time in front of her. But Beth would still be with her. She understood that now.

Mrs. Paganini's excited voice broke through to her. "There was only one empty seat in the auditorium," she declared.

"We'll have a lovely big check to send to the famine relief fund," Eliza answered, and went to change into her regular clothes. When she pulled the scarlet jumper over her head, she took the tiny star pin out of her costume apron and stared down at it. Then she pinned it to her jumper where everyone could see it shine.

. . .

Lucy Maud Montgomery

THE RETURN OF HESTER

Just at dusk, that evening, I had gone upstairs and put on my muslin gown. I had been busy all day attending to the strawberry preserving — for Mary Sloane could not be trusted with that — and I was a little tired and thought it was hardly worthwhile to change my dress, especially since there was nobody to see or care, since Hester was gone. Mary Sloane did not count.

But I did it, because Hester would have cared if she had been here. She always like to see me neat and dainty. So, although I was tired and sick at heart, I put on my pale blue muslin and dressed my hair.

At first I did my hair up in a way I had always liked, but had seldom worn because Hester had disapproved of it. It became me, but I suddenly felt as if it were disloyal to her, so I took the puffs down again and arranged my hair in the plain, old-fashioned way she had liked. My hair, though it had a good many gray threads in it, was thick and long and brown still; but that did not matter — nothing mattered since Hester was dead and I had sent Hugh Blair away for the second time.

The Newbridge people all wondered why I had not put on mourning for Hester. I did not tell them it was because Hester had asked me not to. Hester had never approved of mourning. She said that if the heart did not mourn, crape would not mend matters, and if it did there was no need of the external trappings of woe. She told me calmly, the night before she died, to go on wearing my pretty dresses just as I had always worn them, and to make no difference in my outward life because of her going.

"I know there will be a difference in your inward life," she said wistfully.

And oh, there was! But sometimes I wondered uneasily, feeling almost conscience-stricken, whether it were *wholly* because Hester had left me — whether it were not partly because, for a second time, I had shut the door of my heart in the face of love at her bidding.

When I had dressed, I went downstairs to the front door and sat on the sandstone steps under the arch of the Virginia creeper. I was all alone, for Mary Sloane had gone to Avonlea.

It was a beautiful night; the full moon was just rising over the wooded hills, and her light fell through the poplars into the garden before me. Through an open corner on the western side I saw the sky all silvery blue in the afterlight. The garden was very beautiful just then, for it was the time of the roses and ours were all out — so many of them — great pink, and red, and white, and yellow roses.

Hester had loved roses and could never have enough of them. Her favorite bush was growing by the steps, all gloried over with blossoms — white, with pale pink hearts. I gathered a cluster and pinned it loosely on my breast. But my eyes filled as I did so — I felt so very, very desolate.

I was all alone, and it was bitter. The roses, much as I loved them, could not give me sufficient companion-ship. I wanted the clasp of a human hand, and the love-light in human eyes. And then I fell to thinking of Hugh, although I tried not to.

I had always lived alone with Hester. I did not re-member our parents, who had died in my babyhood. Hester was fifteen years older than I, and she had always seemed more like a mother than a sister. She had been very good to me and had never denied me anything I wanted, save the one thing that mattered.

I was twenty-five before I ever had a lover. This was not, I think, because I was more unattractive than other women. The Merediths had always been the "big" family of Newbridge. The rest of the people looked up to us, because we were the granddaughters of old Squire Meredith. The Newbridge young men would have thought it no use to try to woo a Meredith.

I had not a great deal of family pride, as perhaps I should be ashamed to confess. I found our exalted position very lonely, and cared more for the simple joys of friendship and companionship that other girls had. But Hester possessed it in a double measure; she never allowed me to associate on a level of equality with the young people of Newbridge. We must be very nice and kind and affable to them — *noblesse oblige*, as it were — but we must never forget that we were Merediths.

When I was twenty-five, Hugh Blair came to Newbridge, having bought a farm near the village. He was a stranger, from Lower Carmody, and so was not imbued with any preconceptions of Meredith superiority. In his eyes I was just a girl like others — a girl to be wooed and won by any man of clean life and honest heart. I met him at a little Sunday-school picnic over at Avonlea, which I attended because of my class. I thought him very handsome and manly. He talked to me a great deal, and at last he drove me home. The next Sunday evening he walked up from church with me.

Hester was away or, of course, this would never have happened. She had gone for a month's visit to distant friends.

In that month I lived a lifetime. Hugh Blair courted me as the other girls in Newbridge were courted. He took me out driving and came to see me in the evenings, which we spent for the most part in the garden. I did not like the stately gloom and formality of our old Meredith parlor, and Hugh never seemed to feel at ease there. His broad shoulders and hearty laughter were oddly out of place among our faded, old-maidish furnishings.

Mary Sloane was very much pleased at Hugh's visit. She had always resented the fact that I had never had a "beau," seeming to think it reflected some slight or disparagement upon me. She did all she could to encourage him.

But when Hester returned and found out about Hugh, she was very angry — and grieved, which hurt me far more. She told me that I had forgotten myself and that Hugh's visits must cease.

I had never been afraid of Hester before, but I was afraid of her then. I yielded. Perhaps it was very weak of me, but then I was always weak. I think that was why Hugh's strength had appealed so to me. I needed love and protection. Hester, strong and self-sufficient, had never felt such a need. She could not understand. Oh, how contemptuous she was.

I told Hugh timidly that Hester did not approve of our friendship and that it must end. He took it quietly enough, and went away. I thought he did not care much, and the thought selfishly made my own heartache worse. I was very unhappy for a long time, but I tried not to let Hester see it, and I don't think she did. She was not very discerning in some things.

After a time I got over it; that is, the heartache ceased

to ache all the time. But things were never quite the same again. Life always seemed rather dreary and empty, in spite of Hester and my roses and my Sunday school.

I supposed that Hugh Blair would find himself a wife elsewhere, but he did not. The years went by and we never met, although I saw him often at church. At such times Hester always watched me very closely, but there was no need of her to do so. Hugh made no attempt to meet me, or speak with me, and I would not have permitted it if he had. But my heart always yearned after him. I was selfishly glad he had not married, because if he had I could not have thought and dreamed of him — it would have been wrong. Perhaps, as it was, it was foolish; but it seemed to me that I must have something, if only foolish dreams, to fill my life.

At first there was only pain in the thought of him, but afterward a faint, misty little pleasure crept in, like a mirage from a land of lost delight.

Ten years slipped away thus. And then Hester died. Her illness was sudden and short; but before she died, she asked me to promise that I would never marry Hugh Blair.

She had not mentioned his name for years. I thought she had forgotten all about him.

"Oh, dear sister, is there any need of such a promise?" I asked, weeping. "Hugh Blair does not want to marry me now. He never will again."

"He has never married — he has not forgotten you,"

she said fiercely. "I could not rest in my grave if I thought you would disgrace your family by marrying beneath you. Promise me, Margaret."

I promised. I would have promised anything in my power to make her dying pillow easier. Besides, what did it matter? I was sure that Hugh would never think of me again.

She smiled when she heard me, and pressed my hand.

"Good little sister — that is right. You were always a good girl, Margaret — good and obedient, though a little sentimental and foolish in some ways. You are like our mother — she was always weak and loving. I took after the Merediths."

She did, indeed. Even in her coffin her dark, handsome features preserved their expression of pride and determination. Somehow, that last look of her dead face remained in my memory, blotting out the real affection and gentleness that her living face had almost always shown me. This distressed me, but I could not help it. I wished to think of her as kind and loving, but I could remember only the pride and coldness with which she had crushed out my newborn happiness. Yet I felt no anger or resentment toward her for what she had done. I knew she had meant it for the best — my best. It was only that she was mistaken.

And then, a month after she had died, Hugh Blair came to me and asked me to be his wife. He said he had always loved me, and could never love any other woman.

All my old love for him reawakened. I wanted to say yes — to feel his strong arms about me, and the warmth of his love enfolding and guarding me. In my weakness I yearned for his strength.

But there was my promise to Hester — that promise given by her deathbed. I could not break it, and I told him so. It was the hardest thing I had ever done.

He did not go away quietly this time. He pleaded and reasoned and reproached. Every word of his hurt me like a knife-thrust. But I could not break my promise to the dead. If Hester had been living, I would have braved her wrath and her estrangement and gone to him. But she was dead and I could not do it.

Finally he went away in grief and anger. That was three weeks ago — and I sat alone in the moonlit rose-garden and wept for him. But after a time my tears dried and a very strange feeling came over me. I felt calm and happy, as if some wonderful love and tenderness were very near me.

And now comes the strange part of my story — the part that will not, I suppose, be believed. If it were not for one thing, I think I should hardly believe it myself. I should feel tempted to think I had dreamed it. But because of that one thing I know it was real. The night was very calm and still. Not a breath of wind stirred. The moonshine was the brightest I had ever seen. In the middle of the garden, where the shadow of the poplars did not fall, it was almost as bright as day. One could have read fine print. There was still a little rose glow in the west, and over the airy boughs of the tall poplars one or two large bright stars were shining. The air was sweet with a hush of dreams, and the world was so lovely that I held my breath over its beauty.

Then, all at once, down at the far end of the garden, I saw a woman walking. I thought at first that it must be Mary Sloane; but as she crossed a moonlit path, I saw it was not our old servant's stout, homely figure. This woman was tall and erect.

Although no suspicion of the truth came to me, something about her reminded me of Hester. Hester had liked to wander about the garden in the twilight. I had seen her thus a thousand times.

I wondered who the woman could be. Some neighbor, of course. But what a strange way for her to come! She walked up the garden slowly in the poplar shade. Now and then she stooped, as if to caress a flower, but she plucked none. Halfway up she came out into the moonlight and walked across the plot of grass in the center of the garden. My heart gave a great throb and I stood up. She was quite near to me now — and I saw that it was Hester.

I can hardly say just what my feelings were at this moment. I know that I was not surprised. I was frightened and yet I was not frightened. Something in me shrank back in a sickening terror; but *I*, the real I, was not frightened. I knew that this was my sister, and that there could be no reason why I should be frightened of her, because she loved me still, as she had always done. Further than this I was not conscious of any coherent thought, either of wonder or attempt at reasoning.

Hester paused when she came to within a few steps of me. In the moonlight I saw her face quite plainly. It wore an expression I had never before seen on it — a humble, wistful, tender look. Often in life Hester had looked lovingly, even tenderly, upon me, but always, as it were, through a mask of pride and sternness. This was gone now, and I felt nearer to her than ever before. I knew suddenly that she understood me. And then the half-conscious awe and terror some part of me had felt vanished, and I only realized that Hester was here, and that there was no terrible gulf of change between us.

Hester beckoned to me and said, "Come."

I stood up and followed her out of the garden. We walked side by side down our land, under the willows and out to the road, which lay long and still in that bright, calm moonshine. I felt as if I were in a dream, moving at the bidding of a will not my own, which I could not have disputed even if I had wished to do so. But I did not wish it; I had only the feeling of a strange, boundless content.

We went down the road between the growths of

young fir that bordered it. I smelled their balsam as we passed, and noticed how clearly and darkly their pointed tops came out against the sky. I heard the tread of my own feet on little twigs and plants in our way, and the trail of my dress over the grass; but Hester moved noiselessly.

Then we went through the Avenue — that stretch of road under the apple trees that Anne Shirley, over at Avonlea, calls "The White Way of Delight." It was almost dark here, and yet I could see Hester's face just as plainly as if the moon were shining on it; and whenever I looked at her she was always looking at me with that strangely gentle smile on her lips.

Just as we passed out of the Avenue, James Trent overtook us, driving. It seems to me that our feelings at a given moment are seldom what we would expect them to be. I simply felt annoyed that James Trent, the most notorious gossip in Newbridge, should have seen me walking with Hester. In a flash I anticipated all the annoyance of it; he would talk of the matter far and wide.

But James Trent merely nodded and called out,

"Howdy, Miss Margaret. Taking a moonlight stroll by yourself? Lovely night, ain't it?"

Just then his horse suddenly swerved, as if startled, and broke into a gallop. They whirled around the curve of the road in an instant. I felt relieved, but puzzled. *James Trent had not seen Hester.*

Down over the hill was Hugh Blair's place. When we

came to it, Hester turned in at the gate. Then, for the first time, I understood why she had come back, and a blinding flash of joy broke over my soul. I stopped and looked at her. Her deep eyes gazed into mine, but she did not speak.

We went on. Hugh's house lay before us in the moonlight, grown over by a tangle of vines. His garden was on our right, a quaint spot, full of old-fashioned flowers growing in a sort of disorderly sweetness. I trod on a bed of mint, and the spice of it floated up to me like the incense of some strange, sacred, solemn ceremonial. I felt unspeakably happy and blessed.

When we came to the door, Hester said, "Knock, Margaret."

I rapped gently. In a moment Hugh opened it. Then that happened by which, in after days, I was to know that this strange thing was no dream or fancy of mine. Hugh looked not at me, but past me.

"Hester!" he exclaimed, with human fear and horror in his voice.

He leaned against the doorpost, the big, strong fellow, trembling from head to foot.

"I have learned," said Hester, "that nothing matters in all God's universe, except love. There is no pride where I have been and no false ideals."

Hugh and I looked into each other's eyes, wondering, and then we knew that we were not alone.

• • •

Michael Bedard

Resurrection

At night the dancers and the moon rise
And tie silver bows on silver slippers,
And dance for the dead, who also rise.

And if one falls, they will forgive her
The delay in the brief dance
And the broken pirouettes of silver slippers.

"We also all were dancers once,
With golden slippers bowed with gold.
We also all were dancers once.

We danced the flesh away from bone.
Now dance for us, dance on, dance on.
The dark is short and the sleep long."

And if one stops to gather breath,
They will forgive her,
Those who rise and watch from death.

They will forgive her
The delay in the brief dance
And the broken pirouettes of silver slippers.

ABOUT THE CONTRIBUTORS

JOYCE BARKHOUSE is a former teacher who has lived in Charlottetown, Montreal, and most recently, Halifax. Although she had already been writing stories for many years, she was sixty-one when her first book, *George Dawson: The Little Giant*, was published. Since then she has published several other works, including *The Witch of Port LaJoye*, *Anna's Pet*, and *Pit Pony*. She wrote "Haunted Island" especially for this collection.

Born and raised in Toronto, MICHAEL BEDARD worked for several years in the library at the University of Toronto and then as a pressman in a small print shop. Since 1983 he has balanced writing and raising a family full time. His books include *Emily* (illustrated by Barbara Cooney), *A Darker Magic*, *Painted Devil*, and the Governor General's Award-winning *Redwork*. This is the original publication of "Resurrection."

HAZEL BOSWELL (1882-1979) was born in Quebec City and was still a young girl when she first became interested in the folklore and legends of French Canada. Her love for, and understanding of, the culture and traditions of Quebec are apparent in most of her writings, including *Town House, Country House: Recollections of a Quebec Childhood*. "The White Owl" was first published in *Legends of Quebec: From the Land of the Golden Dog* (Toronto: McClelland & Stewart, 1966).

KARLEEN BRADFORD was born in Toronto, but grew up in Argentina. She has lived in many different countries, including Colombia, England, the United States, the Philippines, Brazil, and Germany. Among her books are *The Haunting at Cliff House, The Nine Days Queen,* and *The Stone in the Meadow*. "Who's Invisible Now?" originally appeared in the Winter 1985 issue of *Quarry* magazine.

JEAN BRIEN is a Peterborough, Ontario, editor and writer. She was a staff reporter and columnist for the *Globe and Mail* for a number of years and an instructor at the Ryerson School of Journalism in Toronto. Jean Brien is afraid of ghosts. This is the original publication of "The Girl in the Rose-Colored Shawl."

BRIAN DOYLE's books for young readers have won five major awards. His best-known works include *Angel*

Square, *Easy Avenue*, and *You Can Pick Me Up at Peggy's Cove*. His latest novel, a sequel to *Spud Sweetgrass*, is *Spud in Winter*. "Carrot Cake" is an original story written expressly for this anthology.

Born in England, MONICA HUGHES spent her childhood in Egypt, was educated in London and Edinburgh, and briefly lived in Rhodesia (now Zimbabwe). She immigrated to Canada in 1952 and began writing professionally in 1971. She is best known for her young adult science fiction, including *The Isis Trilogy*, and her fine contemporary novels, such as *Hunter in the Dark*. She wrote "The Haunting of the Orion Queen" for this collection.

ARCHIBALD LAMPMAN was the finest of Canada's late nineteenth-century poets. *Among the Millet and Other Poems*, his first book, appeared in 1888, and was followed by *Lyrics of Earth* in 1895. His third book, *Alcyone*, was published after his death in 1899. "Midnight" originally appeared in *Among the Millet and Other Poems*.

MARIA LEACH was born in Brooklyn, New York, in 1892, but lived in Barrington, Nova Scotia, for much of her life. She died there in 1977 at the age of eighty-five. She was a well-known author, editor, and folklorist and was the compiler of the Funk & Wagnall *Standard*

Dictionary of Folklore, Mythology and Legend. Her books for children include *The Thing at the Foot of the Bed and Other Scary Stories* and *Noodles, Nitwits, and Numbskulls*. "The Ghostly Spools" is reprinted with permission from *Whistle in the Graveyard: Folktales to Chill Your Bones* (New York: Viking Penguin, 1974).

DENNIS LEE is a Toronto editor, critic, and poet. He has written many books for children, including *Alligator Pie, Jelly Belly,* and *The Ice Cream Store*. These books, with the song lyrics he wrote for the TV series *Fraggle Rock*, have earned him thousands of young fans. "There Was a Man" was first published in *Nicholas Knock and Other People* (Toronto: Macmillan, 1974).

JEAN LITTLE was born in Taiwan and was educated at the University of Toronto. Almost blind since birth, she has nevertheless traveled extensively, visiting more than two dozen countries. Her books, which include *Mama's Going to Buy You a Mockingbird* and *From Anna*, have been published in many languages and have won many awards. This is the first publication of "Without Beth."

Charles Edmunds told his story about the haunting of the Mackenzie homestead to ANDREW MACFARLANE for a feature series MacFarlane wrote for the *Toronto Telegram*. With the demise of the *Telegram* in 1971,

MacFarlane taught journalism at the University of Western Ontario. He is now retired.

Raised in Cavendish, Prince Edward Island, and educated at Prince of Wales College and Dalhousie University, L. M. MONTGOMERY was earning money with her pen by the late 1890s. Her first novel, *Anne of Green Gables*, became an instant best-seller when it was published in 1908 and today "Anne of Green Gables" is a well-known trademark. In 1911 she married Reverend Ewan Macdonald and moved to a small town in Ontario. "The Return of Hester" originally appeared in *Further Chronicles of Avonlea* (Toronto: Doran, 1920). The story is published here with the permission of Ruth Macdonald and David Macdonald, who are the heirs of L. M. Montgomery.

KIT PEARSON was born in Edmonton and grew up in Alberta and British Columbia. After completing her university degree and traveling, she worked as a children's librarian in Ontario and B.C. She now writes full time in Vancouver. She is the author of several books, including *A Handful of Time*, *The Sky Is Falling*, and *The Lights Go On Again*. "Miss Kirkpatrick's Secret" was written expressly for this anthology.

KEN ROBERTS came to Canada from the United States to study history at McMaster University in Hamilton,

Ontario. He later discovered children's literature and decided to become a children's librarian. He has worked as a storyteller and a puppeteer and has been writing stories for young people since 1981. He currently works for the Hamilton Public Library. Ken Roberts's books include *Crazy Ideas*, *Hiccup Champion of the World*, *Pop Bottles*, and *Past Tense*. This is the first publication of "The Closet."

JAMES F. ROBINSON is a freelance writer who collected his true ghost stories about Eastern Ontario when he was living in Kingston in the 1970s and 1980s. He now lives in Vancouver. "Five Candles on a Coffin" is reprinted with permission from *Amazing Tales from Eastern Ontario* by James F. Robinson (Belleville, Ont.: Mika Publishing, 1987).

SHARON SIAMON was born in Saskatoon, but she spent ten years living in a log house in Northern Ontario. The adventures she had there formed the basis for several of her books, including *Log House Mouse*, *Fishing for Trouble*, and *A Horse for Josie Moon*. "Stairs" was written especially for *The Unseen*.

CAROLE SPRAY was born in Moncton, New Brunswick. A mother of two, she spent many years collecting local folklore and has worked as an elementary school teacher, a children's librarian, and a creative writing instructor. Her poems, stories, and reviews have appeared in various Canadian magazines and she has written a children's book entitled *The Mare's Egg: A New World Folk Tale*. "The Keswick Valley Ghost" was first published in *Will o' the Wisp: Folk Tales and Legends of New Brunswick* by Carole Spray (Fredericton, N.B.: Brunswick Press, 1979).

Although he was born in England, TIM WYNNE-JONES spent his early years in Kitimat and Vancouver, British Columbia, before moving to Ottawa. He studied architecture and fine art before turning to writing full time with the publication of his adult novel *Odd's End*. His books include *The Zoom Trilogy* and the Governor General's Award-winning *Some of the Kinder Planets*. "The Clearing" is reprinted from *Some of the Kinder Planets* (Toronto: Groundwood Books, 1993).

PAUL YEE was born in Saskatchewan, but grew up in Vancouver. He has described writing as a way of discovering his roots and defining what being Chinese Canadian means to him. His books for young people include *The Curses of Third Uncle*; *Teach Me to Fly, Sky Fighter*; *Tales from Gold Mountain*; *Roses Sing on New Snow*; and *Breakaway*. "Spirits of the Railway" originally appeared in *Tales from Gold Mountain* (Toronto: Groundwood Books, 1987).